The proceeds

from the sale of this book go back into the
Houston area in the form of projects and grants
to a wide variety of groups in our community.

Our current projects are:

THE HOSPICE AT THE TEXAS MEDICAL CENTER

HOUSTON MUSEUM OF NATURAL SCIENCE

TEXAS MEDICAL CENTER PARK

THE MUSEUM OF FINE ARTS, HOUSTON

THE MUSEUM OF FINE ARTS, RIENZI

URBAN HARVEST

*This volume would not be possible without
the generosity of our members who enthusiastically
shared their favorite recipes and the dedication of the
cookbook committee who unselfishly tasted them all!*

bright sky press

Box 416, Albany, Texas 76430

10 9 8 7 6 5 4 3 2 1

Library of Congress Cataloging-in-Publication Data

Perennial favorites : portable food from The Garden Club of Houston Bulb and Plant Mart /
compiled by Margaret Wolfe with illustrations by Gay Estes.
p. cm.
Includes index.
ISBN 978-1-933979-08-3 (softcover with flaps : alk. paper) 1. Make-ahead cookery. 2. Entertaining.
I. Wolfe, Margaret, 1945- II. Garden Club of Houston. III. Title.

TX652.P4354 2007
641.5'55—dc22   2007028869

Margaret Wolfe, Editor
Gay Estes, Illustrator
Concept, design and art direction by Cregan Design: Ellen Peeples Cregan, Tutu Somerville
Editorial direction by Lucy Herring Chambers

Printed in China through Asia Pacific Offset

Perennial Favorites

THE GARDEN CLUB OF HOUSTON **BULB AND PLANT MART**

BRIGHT SKY PRESS

table of contents

At The Garden Club of Houston's annual Bulb & Plant Mart, we sell thousands of plants and bulbs of many varieties. Our members provide many of the plants we sell, and sharing information and stories from our gardens is one of the true joys of the Mart. For 65 years, Houston gardeners have braved rain, heat, or cold (and sometimes a combination of each!) to get ideas and materials to make their yards even more beautiful.

Moving plants, demonstrating techniques, gathering bulbs, helping long lines of patient gardeners — everyone works hard for three days. In the early days of the Mart, booth chairmen brought a little something tasty to thank their workers. That custom evolved into to a hospitality room that feeds hundreds of workers each day.

On the way to work the booths, everyone tries to bring something delicious and easy to serve. We all appreciate the take-out convenience and gourmet flair that our city's impressive epicurean centers offer, but nothing beats food made with love to share with friends. Something special happens when busy people take a break from work to enjoy good homemade food.

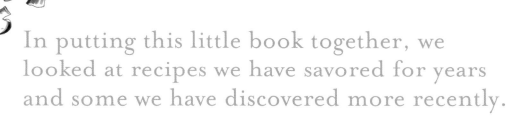

In putting this little book together, we looked at recipes we have savored for years and some we have discovered more recently.

Garden Club members gave us their favorites – some they had on little scraps of paper tucked in their cookbooks and some they knew by heart. We had a wonderful time testing each recipe. For weeks our kitchens were awash with cinnamon, dill, cilantro, chocolate, curry, freshly squeezed orange juice, roasting nuts – every good smell imaginable. What a labor of love!

We tested hundreds of recipes and in the process learned a great deal about ourselves and our Garden Club friends. We like comfort food – we were a little dismayed to find our favorites often contained cream cheese, mayonnaise, sour cream, and cheese, so rest assured you may safely substitute the "lite" version in these recipes and the results will be substantially the same.

We think homegrown and homemade are the best, and we draw many inspirations from the garden. Even nasturtiums make a tasty garnish. Recipes always taste better when we use herbs grown in our own gardens and picked fresh. The fragrances that rise from rosemary, sage, or dill on a sunny day suggest delicious things to eat. But, as much as we enjoy finding culinary inspiration in our garden, many plants and bulbs are poisonous, so we do have to be careful with any horticultural product that we don't specifically know is edible.

We loved the surprise of something that didn't quite turn out like we planned becoming a fabulous new dish, as much as we appreciate the wonder of the bulbs we put out in the fall popping up joyfully in the spring. In the kitchen, as in the garden, there is always room for innovation.

Nothing is more nurturing than taking the time to break bread with friends, old or new. We have so enjoyed putting this little collection together. We hope you take joy in these recipes that have delighted generations of industrious gardeners and hope they become your Perennial Favorites, too.

soups

Asparagus Soup

Mariposa Soup

Lester's Favorite Cucumber Dill Soup

Cream of Pea Soup

Gazpacho

Gazpacho Montrose

Cucumber Gazpacho

Cream of Curry Soup

Curried Avocado Soup

Avocado Cucumber Soup

V-8 Soup

Creamy Spinach Cooler

Spinach Soup

Mulligatawny Soup

Summer Squash Soup

Poblano Soup

Vichyssoise Vert

Ginger Carrot Soup

Cold Cantaloupe Soup

Italian Carrot Soup

Red Pepper Soup

asparagus soup

THIS IS A FAVORITE FROM THE
COMMANDER'S PALACE RESTAURANT
IN NEW ORLEANS.

2 tablespoons unsalted butter
1/2 onion, diced
2 green onions, diced
4 cups chicken stock
1 pound asparagus, washed
2 cups cream
1 teaspoon salt
1/2 teaspoon freshly ground black pepper

Melt butter in a skillet and sauté white and green onions until transparent. Add stock and bring to a boil. Place asparagus in stock and cook until tender, 8-10 minutes. Reserving 12 asparagus tips, put the rest of the asparagus with the stock in a blender. Cover and blend until smooth. Chill asparagus puree. Stir in cream, salt and pepper to taste and reserved asparagus tips. Serve chilled.

MAKES 6 CUPS

To prepare fresh asparagus, hold each end and break like a stick. The asparagus will break off at the less than wonderful end leaving a perfect spear. No cutting!

mariposa soup

GAY ESTES

1 small garlic clove, peeled and crushed
1/2 teaspoon salt or more to taste
2 cups peeled and chopped seedless
   cucumbers (about 3)
1 1/2 cups buttermilk
1/4 cup fresh mint, plus some for garnish
1 tablespoon red wine vinegar
2 ice cubes

Mash garlic and salt into paste and add to blender. Add 1 1/2 cups cucumbers to blender (reserving 1/2 cup for garnish) along with buttermilk, mint leaves, vinegar and ice cubes; blend until smooth. Garnish with mint leaves and 1/2 cup finely diced cucumbers.

MAKES 4 CUPS

lester's favorite cucumber dill soup

CARLA OHLS

3 medium cucumbers, peeled,
  seeded, and cut into chunks
1 1/2 cups chicken broth
1 cup sour cream
  (use half lite version, half regular)
1/2 cup buttermilk
1/2 cup yogurt
2 1/2 tablespoons white wine vinegar
1 garlic clove, minced
2 green onions, sliced thin
Salt to taste
2 tablespoons dill, chopped

Process cucumber chunks in food processor
with 1/2 cup of chicken broth. Do not
over-blend. In a large bowl, combine all
remaining ingredients, including the
cucumbers. Mix well and chill thoroughly.

MAKES 5 CUPS

*You can add toasted slivered almonds,
shrimp or chopped tomatoes,
but this soup is yummy on its own.*

cream of pea soup

LUCY CHEADLE

3 cups fresh peas, or frozen
1 pint water
Dash of sugar
1/2 cup chopped onion
3 tablespoons butter
3 tablespoons flour
1/2 teaspoon salt
Dash of black pepper
3 cups milk
1/2 cup chopped fresh mint
Snipped chives

Cook peas in water with sugar in a
saucepan until soft but still bright green.
Blend onions, peas, and liquid in a blender.
Melt butter in a heavy saucepan; add flour,
salt and pepper and cook, stirring constantly,
until bubbly. Add milk, cook and stir
until smooth. Add pea mixture and heat
slowly. Let cool and refrigerate overnight
so that soup is served cold. Top with fresh
chopped mint and chives.

MAKES 6 CUPS

gazpacho

RENVIA LANDER

3 medium cucumbers, peeled and cut in chunks
3 cups sour cream or yogurt
3 tablespoons white vinegar
2 tomatoes, peeled and chopped
3/4 cup toasted almonds
3 cups chicken broth
2 teaspoons garlic salt
1/2 cup sliced green onions
1/2 cup parsley, chopped

Whirl cucumber in blender with a little chicken broth. Combine with remaining broth, sour cream (or yogurt), vinegar, and garlic salt, stirring just to mix. Chill. Sprinkle tomatoes, almonds, onion, and parsley on top.

SERVES 8

gazpacho montrose

KAY EBERT

5 large, ripe tomatoes, peeled and seeded
1 cucumber, peeled and cut into chunks
1/2 cup chopped green pepper
2 tablespoons lime juice
1 large ripe avocado
2 tablespoons grated onion
5 tablespoons sherry wine vinegar
1/2 teaspoon dill
1 cup tomato juice
Tabasco to taste
Freshly ground black pepper, to taste
Sour cream to garnish

Combine ingredients in blender and serve cold, garnished with sour cream.

SERVES 6

English hot house cucumbers take the deseeding drudgery out of perennial favorite cucumber recipes.

cucumber gazpacho
PAULE JOHNSTON

3 cups chicken broth
3 medium cucumbers, peeled and diced
   (I leave some of the peel on when I use
   the French cucumbers.)
3 cups sour cream (or mix 1 1/2 cups sour
   cream with 1 1/2 cups yogurt)
3 tablespoons white vinegar or
   apple cider vinegar
3 cloves garlic, chopped
2 teaspoons salt to taste
1/2 teaspoon white pepper

Combine all ingredients in blender. If you
need to, blend in batches. Use a container
that holds 9 cups, and chill at least 4 hours
before serving. This lasts about 5 days in the
refrigerator.

SERVES 6

SUGGESTED GARNISHES:
*Chopped sautéed almonds, chopped
parsley, diced tomatoes, chopped
green onions, green pepper or red pepper, avocado
(serve immediately), black olives, mushrooms,
croutons — whatever tickles your fancy!*

cream of curry soup
MARGOT CATER

3 cups yogurt
3 cups chicken or beef consommé
1 clove garlic
1 1/2 teaspoons curry powder
Minced chives

Mix all ingredients except chives in blender.
Chill. Serve very cold with minced chives.
Soup will keep for days in refrigerator and is
low calorie. You can add chicken or shrimp.

SERVES 6

curried avocado soup
JOAN HOWARD

1 ripe avocado
2 cups chicken broth
White pepper
1 cup milk or cream
1 teaspoon curry powder, or more to taste
Fresh chives to garnish
1 lime to garnish

Mix in blender. Serve cold with thin lime
slices and chives on top.

SERVES 4

avocado cucumber soup

DANA PARKEY

2 1/2 cups plain yogurt
2 cups half-and-half
Salt and white pepper to taste
1/2 avocado, finely diced
3 cucumbers, peeled, seeded, and finely diced
1 tablespoon grated onion
1 cup cold chicken broth

Combine yogurt, cream, salt, and pepper
in blender or food processor. Blend well.
Add avocados, cucumbers, onion, and
chicken broth. Chill overnight.

SERVES 6

*Serve very cold with condiments such
as chopped chives, finely chopped
crisp bacon, toasted almonds, or
chopped tomato sprinkled on top.*

V-8 soup

SALLY AVERY

46 ounces V-8 Juice (1 large can or bottle)
1 cup sour cream
1 bunch green onions
2 tablespoons lemon juice
Chopped fresh basil

Blend, chill, and serve.

SERVES 6

*This is easy and elegant.
Serve in demitasse cups with
snipped basil as a garnish.*

creamy spinach cooler

CATHERINE CAGE BRUNS

1 package (10 ounces) frozen chopped
  spinach
2 tablespoons butter or margarine
3 tablespoons flour
1 envelope instant chicken broth or
  1 teaspoon granulated chicken bouillon
1/2 teaspoon salt
1/8 teaspoon pepper
2 cups milk
1 large can (12 ounces) evaporated milk
1 small onion chopped fine (1/4 cup)
1 tablespoon lemon juice

Unwrap spinach and let stand at room
temperature while making sauce. Melt butter
or margarine in a medium size saucepan;
stir in flour, chicken broth, salt and pepper.
Cook, stirring constantly until bubbly.
Stir in milk and evaporated milk; continue
cooking and stirring until sauce thickens and
boils for 1 minute. Remove from heat.
Cut partly thawed spinach into 1/2-inch
pieces and stir into hot sauce until completely
thawed. Stir in onion and lemon juice. Pour
soup into a blender and blend till smooth.
Chill for several hours or overnight.

SERVES 4

spinach soup

JOAN HOWARD

1 package (10 ounces) frozen chopped
  spinach, cooked and drained well
3 tablespoons melted butter
1 cup+ milk
2 teaspoons chopped onion
1 cup cream
1 teaspoon lemon juice
1 1/2 tablespoons chicken bouillon

Combine in blender. Serve chilled.

SERVES 4

*Try finely grated provolone cheese
and crumbled bacon on top.*

mulligatawny soup
ADRIENNE BULLARD

5 cups strong chicken stock
I cup beef stock
I cup heavy cream
I/4 cup apple juice
4 teaspoons curry powder
I tablespoon sherry

Combine chicken stock and beef stock in pan
with heavy cream. Heat, but do not boil. Stir
in apple juice and curry powder. Cool. Add
a tablespoon (or more to taste) of sherry.
Chill. Serve with peeled and finely minced
apples, acidulated with lemon juice on top.

SERVES 6

summer squash soup
BETTY KYLE MOORE

3 or 4 small yellow squash or zucchini
I/2 bell pepper, chopped
I medium onion, chopped
I can (10.5 ounces) chicken broth
   (fresh is better)
3 sprigs parsley
I/4 teaspoon dried dill
   (or 3/4 teaspoon fresh dill)
Salt and pepper
I scant cup of sour cream
I jalapeño, seeded

Combine squash or zucchini, bell pepper,
onion, and chicken broth and cook for
20 minutes. Put in blender and add parsley,
dill, salt and pepper, sour cream, and
jalapeño. Blend until creamy and smooth.
Serve hot or cold.

SERVES 4

poblano soup

RUE JUDD

3 – 4 large poblanos
1/2 of a large Texas 1015 onion,
   coarsely diced
1/4 cup butter
4 tablespoons flour
1 quart chicken broth
1 cup milk
Salt to taste
Freshly, finely ground black pepper
1 jalapeño (optional)

Roast the poblanos under the oven broiler, until the skins blister and blacken, turning 3 or 4 times to catch all sides of the peppers. Remove the peppers to a plastic bag or a bowl with tightly sealing plastic wrap, to steam for about 5 minutes. The blistered skins will now slide off easily. Peel, remove the seeds and stems, and chop coarsely.

While the peppers are toasting, sauté the chopped onion until translucent. Sprinkle the onion and butter with the flour, and stir to make a roux, but do not brown. Add the chicken broth and stir until smooth. Add the chopped peppers.

Puree using a hand-held blender-on-a-stem, or puree in a food processor. Add salt and pepper to taste, and some finely chopped fresh jalapeño if you like the heat.

SERVES 6

Garnish individual servings with your choices of: snipped fresh cilantro; snipped chives; diced avocado; crumbled queso fresca; grated jack cheese; a few lumps of fresh crab meat; sour cream; toasted chopped pecans; toasted pumpkin seeds; or crisp tortilla strips or crumbles.

ginger carrot soup

SARAH MCMURREY

2 tablespoons butter
2 teaspoons freshly minced ginger
1 pound carrots, thinly sliced
1/2 cup leeks, white part only, sliced
3 cups chicken broth
1 cup fresh orange juice
Dash salt and white pepper
Fresh chives or parsley, chopped

Melt butter in saucepan. Add ginger, carrots, and leeks. Sauté until leeks are soft. Add 2 cups chicken broth, cover and simmer for 30 minutes. Remove from heat and puree in blender or with blending stick. Add remaining chicken broth and orange juice to taste. Garnish with chives or snipped parsley. Serve hot or cold.

MAKES 5 CUPS

vichyssoise vert

VIRGINIA ELVERSON

2 tablespoons butter
3 leeks, white part, sliced (about 2 1/2 cups)
1 medium onion, sliced (about 2/3 cup)
2 tablespoons water
4 potatoes, peeled and sliced
    (about 1 1/4 pounds)
3 cups chicken broth
2 1/2 teaspoons salt (or to taste)
1 (10 ounce) package frozen spinach or
    fresh spinach to make a 3/4 cup puree
2 cups half-and-half
1/2 teaspoon ground white pepper
1/8 teaspoon grated nutmeg

In a large heavy saucepan, melt butter and add leeks, onion, and water. Cover and cook over low heat until soft but not brown (about 1/2 hour). Add potatoes, broth, and salt. Cover and cook until potatoes are very tender.

Meanwhile, cook spinach and drain well. Puree in blender or processor until very smooth. Set aside. When potatoes are tender, puree until very fine. Add spinach puree, half-and-half, pepper, and nutmeg. Cool to room temperature. Taste to correct seasonings. Serve chilled.

SERVES 6

cold cantaloupe soup

SARAH MCMURREY

1 large cantaloupe, cut into 1-inch pieces
Juice of two limes
1 teaspoon honey
1 tablespoon frozen orange juice concentrate
3/4 to 1 cup half-and-half
Mint leaves or diced fresh strawberries
   for garnish

Peel, seed, and cut up cantaloupe. Puree in blender or food processor. Add lime juice, honey, and orange juice concentrate. Blend until smooth. Measure puree; use 1/2 the amount of half-and-half as puree. Stir until blended. Serve chilled with mint or strawberry garnish.

SERVES 4

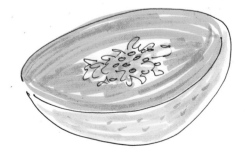

italian carrot soup

ELLEN WILKERSON

4 tablespoons butter
1 medium onion, chopped (about 3/4 cup)
4 large carrots, peeled and chopped
   (about 1 cup)
1 small turnip, peeled and chopped
   (about 1/3 cup)
12 coriander seeds, crushed
Salt to taste
Ground white pepper to taste
2 pints chicken broth
1/4 teaspoon dried marjoram
1/4 teaspoon dried thyme
1/4 teaspoon dried chervil

For garnish:
1/2 cup chopped fresh herbs, such as a combination of chives, parsley, chervil, marjoram, and thyme.

In a heavy saucepan, melt butter. Add onion, carrots, turnip, and coriander seeds. Season lightly with salt and pepper. Cover; simmer gently for 20 minutes. Add chicken broth and herbs. Bring to boil; simmer for 12 minutes. Puree in batches, and return to saucepan; bring again to boil. Correct seasonings and consistency, if necessary.

MAKES 1 1/2 QUARTS

red pepper soup

SUSIE MORRIS

1 tablespoon butter
6 red bell peppers, seeded and cut into
    1/2-inch pieces (about 4 cups)
2 large thinly sliced onions (about 2 cups)
2 cups rich chicken stock
2 cups sour cream (or 1 cup lite sour cream
    and 1 cup buttermilk for lower fat)
1/4 teaspoon salt, or to taste

Butter heavy saucepan. Place vegetables in
pan. Cover with buttered wax paper and lid.
Cook vegetables over low heat until tender
(about 45 minutes). Puree in food processor.
Cool to room temperature. Add chicken
stock, sour cream, and salt. Stir until smooth.
Chill 2 to 4 hours.

MAKES 1 1/2 QUARTS

How to attract honey from
the flower of the world —

that is my everyday business.
I am busy as a bee about it.

Henry David Thoreau,
Journal: August 7, 1851

salads

Quick Niçoise Salad

Nantucket Bleu Spinach Salad

Pepper Salad

Golden Slaw

Curried Chicken and Rice Salad

Chicken Avocado Salad

Texas Tabbouleh

Marinated Shrimp Salad

Mango Jicama Salad

Mango Shrimp Salad

Curried Vegetable Salad

Black Bean Salad

Tuscon Black Bean Salad

Tomato Aspic

Melon in Rum Lime Sauce

Herb's Fruit Salad Dressing

Tomato and Cannellini Bean Salad

Paella Salad

Fantastic Potato Salad

Panzanella

Tuna Salad

Montecito Szechuan Pasta Salad

Tomatoes Caprese

Noodles Japonica

Chinese Chicken Salad

Barrie's Chicken Salad

Spinach Vegetable Salad

Champagne Vinaigrette Pasta Salad

Salade Provençal

quick niçoise salad

MARY HAYES

1 head Romaine lettuce
1 can (12 ounce) solid tuna in water, drained
   and rinsed (or, even better, freshly grilled
   tuna fillets)
1 avocado
5-7 radishes, sliced
1/2 pound green beans, blanched, and chilled
2 hard boiled eggs, sliced

Toss with Niçoise Dressing (see below), or
layer ingredients on a bed of Romaine and
drizzle dressing to taste.

niçoise dressing
1 tablespoon Dijon mustard
3 tablespoons white wine vinegar
1/3 cup olive oil
Salt and pepper

SERVES 4

nantucket bleu
spinach salad

CLARE BRUCE

2 bunches leaf spinach, stemmed,
   washed, and dried well
1 pint fresh blueberries
2/3 cup blue cheese, crumbled
1/2 cup chopped pecans, toasted

nantucket dressing
1 green onion, minced
1/2 pint fresh blueberries
1 teaspoons salt
3 tablespoons sugar
1/3 cup raspberry vinegar
1 cup vegetable oil

Combine green onion, blueberries, salt,
sugar, and vinegar and oil. Pour over salad
and toss.

SERVES 4

pepper salad

MARY LOU SWIFT

1 red onion
2 red bell peppers
2 yellow bell peppers
3 tablespoons olive oil
2 large zucchini, sliced
2 garlic cloves, sliced
1 tablespoon balsamic vinegar
1 can (3/4 ounce) anchovy fillets, chopped
1/4 cup pitted ripe black olives, sliced
1 tablespoon fresh basil, chopped
Salt and pepper

Cut the onion into wedges. Core and seed
the bell peppers then cut into thick slices.
Heat the oil in a large, heavy-bottomed skillet.
Add the onion, bell peppers, zucchini, and
garlic. Cook gently for about 20 minutes,
stirring occasionally. Add the vinegar,
anchovies, and olives. Season to taste with salt
and pepper. Mix and let cool. Serve with
Tomato Toast (at right).

tomato toast
1 loaf French bread
1 garlic clove, minced
1 tomato, peeled and chopped
2 tablespoons olive oil

Cut bread diagonally into 1/2 inch pieces.
Mix the garlic, tomato, and oil together.
Season to taste and spread thinly over each
slice of bread. Put the bread onto a cookie
sheet and cook at 425° for 5-10 minutes or
until crisp.

SERVES 4

golden slaw

CLARE BRUCE

1 medium cabbage, finely chopped
1 medium onion, finely chopped
3/4 cup sugar, plus 1 tablespoon
1 cup white wine vinegar
1 tablespoon salt
1 tablespoon prepared mustard
1 tablespoon celery seed
1 cup salad oil

Alternate layers of cabbage and onion in a large bowl. Sprinkle 3/4 of a cup of sugar over top. Boil vinegar, 1 tablespoon sugar, salt, mustard, and celery seed. Add salad oil and bring to boil again, stirring constantly. Pour over cabbage and onions. Cover and refrigerate overnight. Drain and serve.

MAKES 3 CUPS

curried chicken and rice salad

BETTY DAVIS

4 chicken breast halves
1 cup rice, uncooked
2 cups chicken broth
2 tablespoons vinegar
1/4 cup soy sauce
1 bunch green onions, tops and bottoms
Chopped celery
1 1/2 cups mayonnaise
1 tablespoon curry powder

Put chicken breasts, breast side down, in a pot, cover with water and 3 teaspoons salt. Bring to a boil, skim, cover and turn off heat. Let stand for 2 hours. Cube breasts and cook rice in broth. Toss chicken, rice, and all other ingredients. Chill and serve with chutney and toasted almonds.

SERVES 6

chicken avocado salad

MARY HAYES

3 cups cooked chicken
3 cups cooked basmati rice (white or brown)
2 avocados peeled, diced, and tossed with
   I tablespoon lemon juice
I/4 cup chopped green onions
I cup mayonnaise or I/2 cup mayonnaise and
   I/2 cup crème fraîche
I/4 cup chopped Italian parsley
I teaspoon salt
Freshly ground pepper

Mix all ingredients and chill. Pass with
Avocado Dressing (see below).

avocado dressing

I large avocado, peeled and mashed
2 tablespoons lemon juice
I I/2 cups crème fraîche
I/2 teaspoon Worcestershire sauce
I–2 teaspoons chopped green onions
2 cloves garlic, minced
I teaspoon salt
Dash cayenne pepper

Place all ingredients in a food processor and
blend until smooth. Serve with thick, crusty
bread and garnish with lemon wedges.

SERVES 6

texas tabbouleh

MARGARET WOLFE

I cup bulgur wheat
2 teaspoons minced garlic
I cup cold water
I I/2 teaspoons salt
I/2 cup fresh lemon juice
I/4 cup fresh lime juice
I teaspoon freshly ground pepper
I/2 cup extra virgin olive oil, divided
2 cups diced tomatoes (can be peeled and
   seeded, but I like just diced)
I cup chopped fresh mint
I cup fresh cilantro, chopped
I I/2 cups fresh parsley, chopped
I large cucumber peeled, seeded, and diced
I/2 cup red onion, minced

Combine bulgur, water, lemon juice, and
I/4 cup olive oil in a large bowl. Cover and
marinate 30 minutes. Fluff with fork. Add
remaining olive oil, mint, parsley, cilantro,
onion, garlic, salt and pepper and toss. Add
tomatoes and cucumber. Let marinate at least
30 minutes before serving.

MAKES ABOUT 7 CUPS

*We added the cilantro to a classic recipe because we
like the pop it gives. This is good as a dip with pita
crisps, a side dish for seafood, or a condiment.*

marinated shrimp

COREY ANDER

1 1/4 cups olive oil
3/4 cup white wine vinegar
1 1/2 teaspoons salt
Ground pepper to taste
2 1/2 teaspoons celery seed
2 1/2 tablespoons capers
2 cloves garlic, crushed
2 pounds cooked, shelled shrimp
3 red onions, thinly sliced
Bay leaves, crushed if dried
1 chopped fresh jalapeño (optional)

Mix oil, vinegar, salt, celery seed, capers, and garlic. Chill. In a glass dish, arrange shrimp and onions in layers, sprinkling bay leaves throughout. Pour marinade over all. Cover and refrigerate for 24 hours before serving.

SERVES 8

mango jicama salad

MARIQUITA MASTERSON

Equal amounts of sliced mango and jicama

dressing:
1/3 cup olive oil
Juice of 1 1/2 limes
1 tablespoon sugar
2 teaspoons salt
1/4 cup cilantro

Put in blender and process until smooth. Chill. When ready to serve, drizzle on mango and jicama and toss well.

MAKES 1 CUP DRESSING

mango shrimp salad

DEBBIE ROBINSON

1 red bell pepper, stemmed,
    seeded, and diced
1 ripe mango, diced
4 green onions, white and green parts,
    sliced on the diagonal
1 1/2 pounds medium shrimp,
    cooked and peeled
2 ripe avocados, diced
Juice of 1/2 lime
3 tablespoons snipped fresh chives,
    for garnish
3 tablespoons fresh mint, chopped

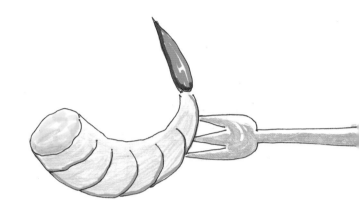

Gently combine the red pepper, mango,
scallions, and shrimp in a large bowl. In a
small bowl, combine the avocado and juice.
Add the avocado to the fruits and vegetables.
Add the fresh mint and just enough Lime
Vinaigrette (see right) to coat the mixture
lightly (you'll have leftover vinaigrette). Taste
and adjust the seasonings. Arrange in a serving
bowl. Scatter the chives over the salad.

lime vinaigrette

1/3 cup fresh lime juice
1 tablespoon Dijon mustard
Salt and pepper to taste
1/4 cup plus 2 tablespoons olive oil
1 green onion, minced
Zest of 1 lime (optional)

Combine all ingredients except oil and
green onions. Whisk in oil, and add green
onions last.

MAKES ABOUT 5 CUPS

curried vegetable salad

GAIL FARIS

I cup rice
I/4 cup French dressing (oil & vinegar type)
I/2 cup mayonnaise
I tablespoon minced onion
3/4 teaspoon curry powder
Salt to taste
I/8 teaspoon pepper
I/2 teaspoon dry mustard
I/2 cup diced celery
I/2 cup thinly sliced radishes
I/2 cup thinly sliced cauliflower
I cup barely cooked peas
   (just defrosted is fine)

The day before, cook rice as directed on package; combine with French dressing and refrigerate. Mix mayonnaise with seasonings and refrigerate. Slice raw vegetables and defrost peas and refrigerate. To serve, toss all together. For an entree type salad, I add shredded chicken.

SERVES 4

black bean salad

JACKIE WALLACE

2/3 cup corn oil
I/2 cup fresh lime juice
6 tablespoons fresh cilantro, chopped
3 tablespoons pickled jalapeño, minced
2 teaspoons minced garlic
I teaspoon ground cumin
I teaspoon salt
3 (19 ounce) cans black beans,
   rinsed and drained
I cup chopped red onion
I cup sweet red pepper, chopped
I cup sweet yellow pepper, chopped

In a large bowl, stir oil, lime juice, cilantro, jalapeño, garlic, cumin, and salt. Add remaining ingredients, toss to coat well. Cover, refrigerate for several hours or overnight. Serve with tortilla chips.

MAKES 8 CUPS

tucson black beans

GAIL FARIS

1 pound dried black beans
  (or 3 cans (15 ounce), rinsed)
2 cloves of garlic
  (1 of them crushed for dressing)
1/4 cup balsamic vinegar
2/3 cup olive oil
Salt and pepper
Juice of 2 lemons
Juice of 1 lime
1 large red pepper, chopped
6 green onions, chopped
1/4 cup fresh cilantro, chopped

For dried beans: Wash beans and place in a pan.
Cover with water and place on high heat to boil.
Boil for 5 minutes and turn off heat. Let stand
for 1 hour. Drain beans and again cover with
water and a few sprigs of cilantro and 1 clove of
garlic. Simmer until tender, about 1 hour.

Drain and rinse cooked or canned beans
and toss with red pepper, green onions,
and chopped cilantro. Mix together vinegar,
crushed clove of garlic, olive oil, and salt and
pepper to taste, and pour over beans. Cover
and let stand in refrigerator at least 4 hours.
Refrigerated, this keeps indefinitely and can
be pureed as a dip for tortilla chips.

MAKES 7 CUPS

tomato aspic

SHERRY KEMPNER

6 cups tomato or V-8 juice
2/3 cup fresh lemon juice
4 tablespoons Worcestershire sauce
Tabasco
4 tablespoons unflavored gelatin
8 ounces cream cheese

Boil 5 cups tomato or V-8 juice, lemon juice, Worcestershire sauce, and dash of Tabasco. Soak unflavored gelatin in 1 cup of the vegetable juice and dissolve into hot mixture. Mix 1 cup of juice mixture with the cream cheese until smooth. Pour cream cheese mixture into a 6-8 cup well-greased mold. Chill.

When firm, pour remaining juice mixture over cream cheese and chill. You can add olives, crab meat, shrimp, or other ingredients to the juice mixture at this time. To serve, unmold and serve with mayonnaise.

SERVES 6-8

melon in rum lime sauce

SARAH BAKER

1 cantaloupe
1 small honeydew melon
1/8 of small watermelon
1 cup fresh blueberries
2/3 cup sugar
1/3 cup water
1 teaspoon lime zest
6 tablespoons fresh lime juice
1/2 cup light rum

Cut the cantaloupe and honeydew melons in half and remove the seeds. With a melon scoop, form the fruit into small balls. Do the same with the watermelon, working around the seeds. Pile the melon balls and the blueberries into a serving bowl and chill. In a small saucepan, mix the sugar with the water; bring to a boil, reduce heat and simmer for five minutes. Add the lime zest, and let cool at room temperature. Stir in the lime juice and rum. Pour the sauce over the melon balls and blueberries, and chill, covered, for several hours.

SERVES 6

Decorate with sprigs of mint and add additional rum, if desired.

herb's fruit salad dressing

HYACINTH BEAN

1/2 cup sugar
I cup water
2 tablespoons chopped fresh ginger or
  I teaspoon grated lime zest and
2 tablespoons fresh lime juice or
  2 tablespoons coarsely chopped fresh basil

Combine sugar and water in a saucepan and boil, over high heat, stirring constantly until sugar is dissolved. Reduce heat to low and add flavorings. Simmer for 10 minutes and strain into glass container. Let cool. Keeps for 3 - 5 days in refrigerator. Great over fruit salad; in drinks, dessert sauces, and tea; or drizzled over pound cake or angel food cake that is covered in fresh fruit.

MAKES 2 CUPS

tomato and cannellini bean salad

ESTHER GLOVER

4 large tomatoes, roughly diced
2 (14-ounce) cans cannellini beans
  (white kidney beans), drained
2 tablespoons shaved red onion
1/2 bunch Italian parsley, chopped
Fresh basil and dill to taste
2 cloves finely minced garlic
1/4 cup olive oil
1/4 cup white balsamic vinegar
Salt and pepper to taste

Combine the tomatoes, beans, herbs, and garlic. Drizzle with olive oil and white balsamic vinegar, and let marinate overnight (red vinegar will discolor the beans).
It's best to salt this salad right before serving to prevent the vegetables from leeching too much liquid. Serve as a hearty salad, or put out crostini and let guests make their own bruschetta.

SERVES 4

paella salad

SARAH MCMURREY

2 cups uncooked white rice
1 thread saffron
2 tablespoons tarragon vinegar
1/3 cup oil
1 teaspoon salt
1/8 teaspoon dry mustard
1 large tomato, seeded and chopped
1/2 cup red onion, finely chopped
1/2 green, red, or yellow bell pepper
1/3 cup celery, thinly sliced
1 tablespoon chopped red pepper
2 cups chicken, cut in bite-sized pieces
1 small jalapeño, seeded and finely chopped

Cook rice with thread of saffron. Mix rice,
vinegar, oil, salt, and mustard and chill.
Add remaining ingredients, toss lightly,
and chill well.

SERVES 6

*You may substitute 1 cup
shrimp or sausage for
1 cup of the chicken.*

fantastic potato salad

LAURIE LIEDTKE

12 medium white potatoes
2 tablespoons cider vinegar
2 tablespoons butter, melted
2 tablespoons sugar
2 teaspoons salt
2 cups celery, chopped
12 hard boiled eggs, sliced
1 cup fresh parsley, minced
2 (4 ounce) jars chopped pimientos
1/2 cup minced onion
1 (10 ounce) jar sweet pickle relish

Boil potatoes in skins till tender. While hot,
peel, cube, and toss potatoes lightly with
vinegar, butter, sugar, and salt. Refrigerate
until thoroughly chilled. Add celery, eggs,
parsley, pimiento, onion, and pickle relish.
Chill until flavors blend. Moisten with
chilled Mayonnaise-Horseradish Sauce
(see below), 1 hour before serving.

mayonnaise-horseradish sauce

1 quart mayonnaise
1 (4 ounce) jar prepared horseradish
Mix well and refrigerate.

SERVES 12

panzanella

MARGARET WOLFE

3 tablespoons olive oil
1 small loaf French bread cut into
   1 inch cubes (6 cups)
1 teaspoon kosher salt
2 large, ripe tomatoes, cut into 1 inch cubes
1 cucumber peeled, seeded, and sliced
   1/2 inch thick
1 red bell pepper, seeded and cut into 1 inch cubes
1 yellow bell pepper, seeded and cut into
   1 inch cubes
1/2 red onion, cut in half and thinly sliced
1/2 cup fresh basil leaves, coarsely chopped
3 tablespoons capers, drained

Heat oil in large sauté pan. Add bread and
salt, cook over low to medium heat, tossing
frequently for 10 minutes or until nicely
browned. In large bowl, mix tomatoes,
cucumber, red pepper, yellow pepper,
red onion, basil, and capers. Add bread
cubes and toss with vinaigrette (see below).
Allow salad to sit for half an hour for
flavors to blend.

vinaigrette

1 teaspoon finely minced garlic
1/2 teaspoon Dijon mustard
3 tablespoon Champagne vinegar
1/2 cup olive oil
1/2 teaspoon kosher salt
1/2 teaspoon freshly ground black pepper

SERVES 8

tuna salad

LOUISE COOLEY

1 can (6 ounce) tuna
Cocktail onions, cut in half
1 cup chow mein noodles
Soy sauce
Curry powder to taste
1/2 cup mayonnaise
1/2 cup frozen baby peas
1/2 cup celery, chopped

Mix tuna, mayonnaise, curry powder, and
a little soy sauce. Before serving, mix in
cocktail onions, noodles, and frozen peas.
Season to taste.

SERVES 6 AS AN APPETIZER

montecito szechuan pasta salad

ESTHER GLOVER

1 (12-16 ounce) package angel hair pasta
1/8 pound snow peas
1 cup mayonnaise
1/3 cup soy sauce
1 tablespoon chili oil
1/8 cup sesame oil
1 1/2 teaspoon Dijon mustard
1 clove garlic
1/4 pound cooked turkey or chicken, diced
1/2 bunch green onions, chopped
1 medium carrot, diced
1/2 can water chestnuts, drained and sliced
1 red bell pepper, diced
1/2 cup white shoe peg corn
1/2 bunch cilantro leaves, chopped
2 tablespoons toasted sesame seeds

Cook the angel hair pasta until al dente, according to package directions. Drain, rinse with cold water. Pull stringy stems off snow peas, and slice on the diagonal into thin strips. Combine the mayonnaise, soy sauce, chili oil, sesame oil, Dijon mustard, and garlic in food processor or blender. Combine the pasta, snow peas, turkey or chicken, green onions, carrot, water chestnuts, bell pepper, and corn in a large bowl. Add mayonnaise dressing to taste and toss. Garnish with sesame seeds and cilantro.

SERVES 6-8

tomatoes caprese salad

ALICE CAPONE

2 pounds ripe tomatoes, diced
1 pound mozzarella, diced
1 cup fresh basil leaves
1/4 cup olive oil, or to taste
Pepper and salt
1 tablespoon fresh oregano
Dash of balsamic vinegar

Chop the tomatoes and the mozzarella.
Season with the olive oil, basil, oregano, and
a little salt and pepper.

SERVES 6

*Fresh mozzarella di bufalo can
sometimes be found at
specialty markets.*

noodles japonica

MARGARET WOLFE

Salt and pepper
3 garlic cloves, minced
3 tablespoons fresh ginger,
  peeled and finely chopped
4 green onions, thinly sliced
1/2 cup chunky-style peanut butter
1/4 cup tahini
2 teaspoons Chinese chili paste
1/4 cup soy sauce
1/4 cup fresh cilantro, minced
  plus some for garnish
1 (8 ounce) package soba noodles
  (Japanese buckwheat pasta)
1 large cucumber, cubed, (3 cups)
3/4 cup cashews, coarsely chopped
2 tablespoons sesame oil
2 tablespoons rice wine vinegar

Add noodles to a pot of boiling water
and a little salt. Stir well. Cook for about
6 minutes or until tender. Drain and rinse
under cold water. In a large bowl, mix garlic,
ginger, and green onions. Mix in the peanut
butter and the tahini, chili paste, soy sauce,
and stir. Add 1/2 cup hot water and stir
into sauce. Toss noodles with sauce and chill,
covered, for several hours or until ready
to serve. Right before serving, toss with
cucumber, cilantro, cashews, sesame oil,
vinegar, and pepper.

SERVES 4-6

chinese chicken salad

SUSAN MICLETTE

8 chicken breast halves
Olive oil
Kosher salt
Freshly ground black pepper
1 pound asparagus, ends removed and
    cut into thirds diagonally
2 red bell peppers, cored and seeded
4 green onions, (white and green parts,
    sliced diagonally)
2 tablespoons white sesame seeds, toasted

Preheat oven to 350°. Bake chicken breasts
with a little olive oil and salt and pepper for
35–40 minutes until the chicken is just
cooked. Cool. Shred chicken in long slim
pieces. Cut asparagus into bite-size pieces
and blanch in pot of boiling salted water for
3-5 minutes until tender. Plunge into ice
water to stop cooking. Drain. (This can be
done the day before and placed in the
refrigerator.) Cut peppers into strips about
the size of asparagus pieces. Combine
shredded chicken, asparagus, and peppers
in large bowl.

chinese chicken salad dressing
1 cup vegetable oil
1 teaspoon ginger, peeled and grated
1/2 cup apple cider vinegar
1 tablespoon white sesame seeds, toasted
1/3 cup soy sauce
1/2 cup smooth peanut butter
3 tablespoons dark sesame oil
4 teaspoons kosher salt
1 tablespoon honey
1 teaspoons freshly ground black pepper
2 garlic cloves, minced

Combine, pour over salad, and toss.

SERVES 6-8

barrie's chicken salad

ELLEN MORRIS

6 cups chicken broth
8 ounces wild rice
1 (2 1/2 pound) roasted chicken
 (store bought is fine), skinned, boned
 and cut into 1/2 inch pieces (about 4 cups)
1 red bell pepper, chopped
2 bunches arugula, chopped
1/4 cup green onion, chopped
3 tablespoons soy sauce
3 tablespoons rice vinegar
3 tablespoons sesame oil
2 cups pecans, toasted and chopped
2 heads romaine lettuce, washed and dried

Bring broth to boil in saucepan. Add rice
and boil, covered, 50 minutes at low heat.
Drain and transfer to large bowl. Mix in
chicken, bell pepper, arugula, and green
onions. Mix soy sauce, vinegar, and oil
in small bowl. Pour over salad and mix
to coat. Season with salt and pepper.
This can be made 4 hours ahead, covered
and chilled. To serve, mix nuts into salad,
place salad in center of plate and surround
with romaine spears.

SERVES 6

spinach vegetable salad

BARBARA BUSH

2 pounds fresh chopped spinach
 (you chop it)
10 hardboiled eggs, sliced
1 pound bacon, cooked and crumbled
1 cup sliced shallots
1 medium head of lettuce, shredded
1 (10 ounce) package thawed frozen peas,
 uncooked
1/2 cup Swiss cheese, grated
2 1/2 cups mayonnaise
2 1/2 cups sour cream
Salt and pepper, to taste
Worcestershire sauce, to taste
Lemon juice, to taste

Layer spinach, eggs, bacon, lettuce, shallots,
and peas in a large salad bowl. Combine the
mayonnaise, sour cream, Worcestershire
sauce, lemon juice, and salt and pepper.
Pour over the salad. Do not toss.
Cover and chill for 12 hours before serving.

SERVES 16

champagne vinaigrette pasta salad

MARGARET ROTAN

1 box (1 pound) tri-colored rotini pasta
8 ounces baby spinach leaves
1 pint tomatoes (I like the grape or cherry
    ones, cut in half if they are too big.)
1 bunch green onions, chopped
1 cup or more feta cheese, crumbled
1 - 2 seedless cucumbers,
    sliced and quartered
1 cup toasted pine nuts

Toss with Champagne Vinaigrette Dressing
(see right). Chill.

champagne vinaigrette dressing

1 cup olive oil
1 cup champagne vinegar
3 cloves garlic, minced
2 - 4 teaspoons Dijon mustard
3/4 cup freshly grated Parmesan cheese
1 teaspoon oregano
Sea salt and freshly ground pepper

SERVES 6

*I like to prepare this the night before,
reserving some of the cut tomatoes,
a handful of pine nuts, and a good
sprinkle of the parmesan cheese
to put on top before serving.*

salade provençal

MARIANNA BREWSTER

1 1/2 cups fresh shell beans
   (flageolets or cannellini or a combination)
5 tablespoons red wine vinegar
5 tablespoons extra virgin olive oil
Salt and freshly ground pepper
3/4 pound green beans, ends removed
3/4 pound yellow beans, ends removed
1/2 pound cherry tomatoes in assorted colors
20 fresh basil leaves

Cover the shell beans with water. Bring to
a boil and cook until tender, about 25
minutes. Drain and toss with 4 tablespoons
vinegar, 5 tablespoons olive oil, salt and
pepper. Keep warm. Blanch the green and
yellow beans in boiling salted water until they
are slightly crisp. Drain and add to shell
beans and toss.

Halve the cherry tomatoes and season
with salt and pepper and the remaining
1 tablespoon of vinegar. Toss.

Place the various beans on a platter and top
with the tomatoes and a spoonful of Garlic
Mayonnaise (see right).

garlic mayonnaise
1/2 cup mayonnaise
1 clove of garlic, smashed
Juice of 1/2 lemon
Heavy cream

Blend mayonnaise, garlic and lemon juice.
Stir in cream to thin.

SERVES 8

sandwiches

Pimiento Cheese
Chicken Salad
Egg Salad
Vegetable
Bollin Party
Curried Chicken

pimiento cheese

1 pound cheddar cheese, grated
1 jar (4 ounce) pimientos, drained
Mayonnaise to taste

Combine in large bowl, chill and serve on
your favorite bread.

MAKES 12 FINGER OR
6 FULL-SIZED SANDWICHES

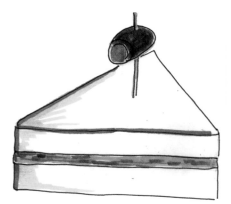

 YOU MIGHT ALSO ADD, TO TASTE:

Mustard, prepared or dried
Fresh or dried dill
Lemon juice (1/4 cup)
Green onions (1/2 cup)
Red onions (1/2 cup)
Bacon
Jalapeños
Sugar (1 teaspoon)
Pecans
Prepared horseradish
   (1 teaspoon)
1 fresh garlic clove,
   finely minced
Worcestershire sauce

Tabasco
Sour cream
Cottage cheese
Provolone cheese
Swiss cheese
1/3 provolone, 1/3 swiss
   and 1/3 cheddar

There are at least
25 variations each year at
the Mart. Pimiento cheese
is everyone's favorite and
everyone has her own recipe.

chicken salad

4 cups diced, cooked chicken
Salt and pepper
2 or more cups mayonnaise
1 cup finely chopped green onions
1 cup diced celery

Combine ingredients and chill.
Serve on lettuce leaf for a salad or on any
good bread for a sandwich.

MAKES 16 FINGER OR
8 FULL-SIZED SANDWICHES

 YOU MIGHT ALSO ADD, TO TASTE:

Chopped fresh parsley   *Chopped olives*
Diced crisp bacon   *Diced apples*
Fresh lemon or lime juice   *Substitute sour cream or yogurt*
Chopped peanuts   *for half or more of the*
Freshly grated or dried ginger   *mayonnaise*
Curry powder (great with ginger)   *Cumin (2 teaspoons)*
Chutney (great with curry   *Chopped fresh jalapeños*
powder and ginger chopped and   *(2 teaspoons…if you like it*
mixed in or on the side)   *fairly hot)*
Red or white grapes, sliced   *Chopped fresh cilantro (1/4 cup)*
Almonds, toasted   *Fresh or dried tarragon (especially*
good with sour cream instead of
mayonnaise)

egg salad

12 hard boiled eggs peeled and chopped
1 cup mayonnaise
1 bunch green onions

Mix chopped egg with mayonnaise and green
onions. Add more mayonnaise to taste.

MAKES 24 FINGER OR
12 FULL-SIZED SANDWICHES

YOU MIGHT ALSO ADD, TO TASTE:

Celery, diced
Jalapeños (1 teaspoon)
Bell pepper, any color
Finely minced garlic
(1 clove finely chopped)
Cilantro (great as garnish or
1 tablespoon, snipped)
Chili powder
Caviar (great as garnish)
Bacon, fried crisp and crumbled
Fresh parsley
Fresh watercress
Freshly squeezed lemon juice
Pickle relish

vegetable sandwiches

NANCY THOMAS

2 small onions, quartered
1 green pepper, quartered
2 medium cucumbers, peeled and quartered
2 carrots, scraped and coarsely chopped
2 stalks celery cut in large pieces
1 cup mayonnaise
2 packages unflavored gelatin
Salt and pepper to taste

Put onions, green pepper, celery, and cucumbers into blender. Turn blender off and on several times to chop vegetables. Add chopped carrots. Finely chop all vegetables but do not puree. Put vegetables in a strainer and allow to drain for several hours. Reserve 1/2 cup of the juice. Put the reserved liquid in a saucepan and heat well but do not boil. Put the gelatin in a cup, and spoon in just enough of the heated liquid to dissolve; then pour dissolved gelatin into the rest of the hot liquid in saucepan. Stir until completely dissolved. Add to vegetable mixture along with 1 cup of mayonnaise and salt and pepper to taste. Mix well. Refrigerate overnight before making into sandwiches.

WILL MAKE ABOUT 80 FINGER SANDWICHES

bollin party sandwiches

URSULA ASTON

9 ounces cream cheese
1 can (4 1/2 ounce) pitted black olives, drained and sliced
6-7 slices crisp bacon, crumbled
1 cup finely chopped toasted pecans
1 cup fresh parsley, chopped
1 small onion, grated
2 teaspoons lemon juice
Salt and pepper, to taste
Mayonnaise for desired consistency

Combine cream cheese, olives, bacon, pecans, parsley, onion, lemon juice, salt and pepper, and mayonnaise. Mix well. Spread filling generously on your favorite bread. Trim crusts and cut into triangles.

MAKES 7 DOZEN SMALL SANDWICHES

curried chicken sandwiches

SIDNEY FAY

4 chicken breast halves (2 whole breasts)
1/2 cup celery
Salt and pepper
1 cup grapes, red or white, sliced
Sliced almonds
1 bunch green onions
1 cup mayonnaise
1 cup sour cream
1 teaspoon curry powder
1 teaspoon tarragon vinegar
1 teaspoon garlic salt
1 teaspoon horseradish
1 teaspoon onion juice
1 jar Chutney

Cook chicken breasts in water with a carrot, celery stick, and an onion. Cool in refrigerator. Cut up chicken and mix with grapes, celery, almonds, and green onions. Combine mayonnaise, curry powder, vinegar, garlic salt, horseradish, and onion juice.

(This is a wonderful dip for vegetables!) Combine curry mixture with sour cream and mix with chicken mixture. Make sandwiches by spreading Chutney on bread and piling on chicken salad.

MAKES 6 FULL-SIZED SANDWICHES

Make plenty!

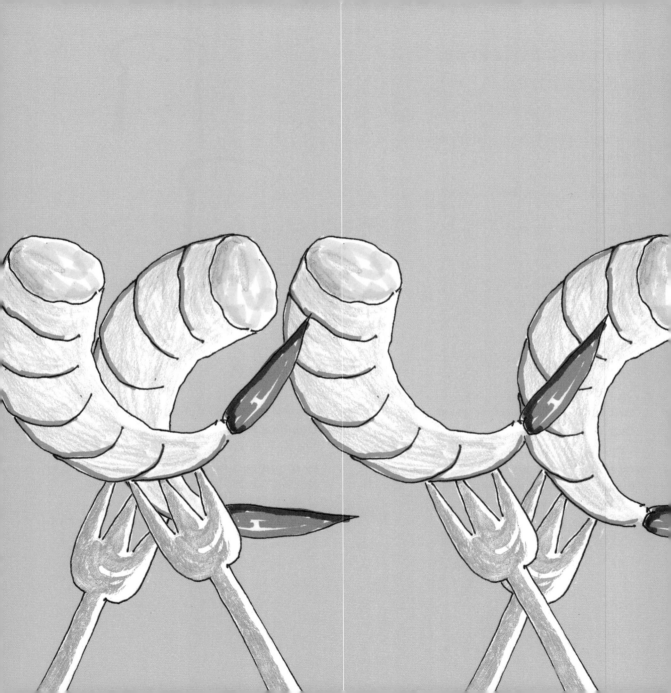

nibbles

Quick Toasties

Mushroom Paté Rienzi

Egg Salad Mold

Leila's Deviled Eggs

Fresh Herb Cheese Log

Zippy Cranberry Appetizer

Chicken Garden Paté

Curried Peanut Chicken

Liz's Chicken Liver Paté

Paté Raj

Anne's Stuffed Celery

Sidney's Favorite Pimiento Cheese Rolls

Felix's Chili Con Queso

Susie's Hearty Queso

Creamy Jalapeño Dip

Cheddar Carousel

Pancho Villa Pie

Tomato Cheese Tartlets

Tzatziki

Cilantro Mousse

Sylvia Bartz' Avocado Mousse

Easy Corn Dip

Mexicorn Dip

Frances' Baked Sweet Onion Dip

Green Chili Dip

Santa Barbara "Caviar"

Mold Marcel

Asian Nuts

Blue, Blue Cheesecake

Green Herb Dip

Spartan Cheese

Sarah's Tortilla Rollups

Teresa's Salmon Mold

Salmon Pizza

Hot Crab Dip

Smoked Trout Dip

Cheesy Spinach Squares

Great Balls of Fire

Rosemary Pecans

Olive Cheese Balls

Cheese Krispies

Longhorn Pecans

Ledbetter Cheese Straws

Herbed Potato Chips

quick toasties

BETTY DAVIS

Butter, melted

Croissants, hot dog buns, French bread sliced, flour tortillas, pita, or bagels—any good bread cut into strips about an inch wide.

Toasted sesame seeds or poppy seeds

Dip bread in melted butter and sprinkle with sesame seeds or poppy seeds. Bake in a 250° oven for 1 1/2 hours.

An imprecise but delicious recipe! Keeps forever.

mushroom pâté rienzi

BETTY CONNER

2 tablespoons butter
8 ounces fresh mushrooms, sliced
1 1/2 teaspoons minced garlic
1/4 cup chopped green onions (white part)
2 tablespoons chopped green onion (green part)
1/3 cup chicken stock
4 ounces cream cheese
1 teaspoon Worcestershire sauce
2 teaspoons fresh lemon juice
1 1/2 teaspoons minced fresh thyme
1 teaspoon salt

Sauté mushrooms in 2 tablespoons butter. Add garlic and 1/4 cup green onions. Sauté 1 minute. Add chicken stock and cook till liquid is absorbed. Cool. Blend cream cheese and 2 tablespoons butter. Add mushroom mixture, 2 tablespoons green onions (green part), Worcestershire, lemon, thyme, salt and pepper. Pour into a 1 cup mold lined with plastic wrap and chill. To serve, remove from mold and place on a serving platter. Garnish with parsley and lemon slices. May be prepared 3 days in advance.

MAKES ABOUT 2 CUPS

egg salad mold

NANCY THOMAS

1 pint sour cream
1/8 teaspoon black pepper
1/2 cup mayonnaise (preferably homemade)
Dash Tabasco
Dash Worcestershire sauce
10–12 hard boiled eggs
1/8 teaspoon curry powder
1/4 cup minced green onion
Salt

Finely chop eggs, add all ingredients except
sour cream. Mix well, spoon into a 5-cup
mold lined with plastic wrap; cover and
chill for at least 3 hours. Unmold onto
serving dish. Ice with well mixed sour cream.
Garnish with parsley and chopped green
onions. Serve with Melba toast or other
crisp toast.

MAKES 5 CUPS

leila's deviled eggs

LEILA HULL

12 hard boiled eggs
1/2 cup sweet pickle relish
2 cups mayonnaise
Salt and pepper

Cut eggs in half vertically. Slice small section
from underneath each egg white for stability,
and place on serving platter. Mix yolks with
mayonnaise, pickle relish, and salt and
pepper to taste. Pipe or spoon yolk mixture
into cooked whites and chill. If you like,
garnish with paprika, caviar, cilantro pesto,
curry powder, or snipped chives.

MAKES 24 DEVILED EGGS

fresh herb cheese log

JEANIE CARTER

1 pound cream cheese, softened
1/2 pound butter, softened
1 teaspoon garlic, mashed
1 1/2 tablespoons sweet marjoram, chopped
1 1/2 tablespoons chives, chopped
1 tablespoon chopped fresh basil
1 teaspoon chopped fresh thyme
1 tablespoon chopped fresh parsley
1/2 teaspoon salt
1/4 teaspoon freshly ground white pepper

Beat cream cheese and butter together. Add mashed garlic, mixing well. Add finely chopped herbs, salt and pepper. Chill slightly and form into logs. Wrap tightly in plastic wrap. Refrigerate or freeze. Serve at room temperature with toast.

MAKES 3 CUPS

zippy cranberry appetizer

ESTHER GLOVER

1/2 cup sugar
1/2 cup packed brown sugar
1 cup water
1 package (12 ounce)
   fresh or frozen cranberries
1 to 3 tablespoons horseradish
1 tablespoon Dijon mustard
1 package (8 ounce) cream cheese, softened
Assorted crackers

In a large saucepan, bring sugars and water to a boil. Stir in cranberries; return to a boil. Cook for 10 minutes or until thickened, stirring occasionally. Cool. Stir in horseradish and mustard. Transfer to a bowl; refrigerate until chilled. Just before serving, spread cream cheese over crackers; top with cranberry mixture, or you can put cream cheese on a serving plate and cover with cranberry mixture.

MAKES 3 CUPS OF CRANBERRY MIXTURE

This is really great as a spread on turkey sandwiches.

chicken garden pâté

LEE COCHRAN

3/4 to 1 cup coarsely chopped yellow onion

6 cups cooked chicken, turkey, or duck meat

1 1/2 cups butter

1/2 to 1 cup cream, as needed

1/3 cup Dijon mustard

1/2 cup fresh herbs: tarragon, sage, lemon
thyme, marjoram, basil, or a combination
of these, chopped

1 to 2 teaspoons Tabasco

Salt to taste

Freshly ground white pepper, to taste

2-3 tablespoons fresh lemon juice

1/2 cup pistachios whole, shelled
and dry-roasted

1/2 cup minced fresh parsley

Process chopped yellow onions, meat, butter, and cream until very smooth. When smooth, add mustard, seasonings, and lemon juice; adjust salt to taste; stir in pistachios. Line a loaf pan or terrine with plastic wrap, being sure to push it into corners. Spoon about a third of meat mixture into the lined pan. Smooth surface, pushing mixture all the way to the edge.

Put a layer of herbs on the meat, leaving a 1/2 inch space around the edges. Carefully add another third of meat mixture, and top with another layer of herbs (at different intervals across surface). Finish with remaining meat mixture. Smooth all the way to the edges; give pan several raps to settle completely. Fold edges of plastic wrap over the top to cover. Refrigerate several hours or overnight until completely firm. Turn out paté onto a serving plate and carefully remove plastic wrap. Smooth out any rough or broken spots. Cover with chopped fresh parsley pressed into sides. Decorate with herbs. Slice into 1/2 inch pieces and serve with toast, crusty bread, or crackers. Serve at room temperature.

MAKES 4 CUPS

curried peanut chicken

CAROLYN DAVIS

2 whole chicken breasts (4 halves),
  skinned and boned
2 cups half-and-half
1 cup mayonnaise
3 tablespoons mango Chutney
2 tablespoons dry sherry
1 tablespoon sherry vinegar
  (or balsamic vinegar)
2 tablespoons plus 1 teaspoon curry powder
1 teaspoon turmeric
2 cups salted and roasted peanuts
Fresh cilantro for garnish
Raisins, for garnish if desired

Place the chicken breasts in a shallow
baking dish just large enough to hold them.
Pour the half-and-half over them and bake at
350° for 30 minutes. Let cool and cut into
bite-sized cubes. Process the mayonnaise,
chutney, sherry, vinegar, curry powder,
and turmeric in a food processor with a
steel blade until blended. Add peanuts
and continue processing until nuts are
finely chopped.

MAKES 32 PORTIONS

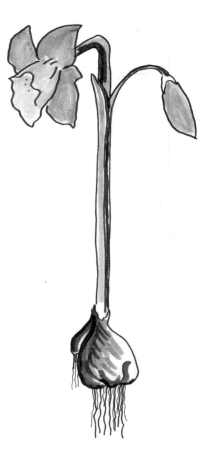

*Serve two ways: Dip the chicken pieces
into the curry mayonnaise mixture with
a small skewer or toothpick and place
on serving plate; or, place chicken bites
next to curry sauce with toothpicks
for dipping. Garnish with cilantro
and raisins, if desired.*

liz's chicken liver pâté

LINDA GRIFFIN

2 onions chopped
1/2 teaspoon garlic, chopped
1 pound of chicken livers, washed
1/4 pound of butter
Salt and pepper
Fresh thyme, rosemary, and bay leaf
Cognac

Sauté onions and garlic in butter. Add chicken livers and sauté over medium high heat until pink. Add salt and pepper and herbs and let cool down. Remove herbs and blend. Add a splash of cognac and correct the seasoning. Put in a 1-cup mold or container, cover with a thin film of clarified butter and chill. Serve with crostini or a good cracker.

MAKES 1 CUP

pâté raj

ADRIENNE BULLARD

6 ounces cream cheese, softened
1 cup grated sharp cheddar cheese
4 teaspoons dry sherry
1/2 teaspoon curry powder
1/4 teaspoon salt (optional)
1 (8 ounce) jar mango Chutney,
    finely chopped
1-2 green onions, chopped

In a large bowl, beat cream cheese, cheddar, sherry, curry powder, and salt. Spread mixture on serving platter about 1/2 inch thick. Chill until firm. At serving time, spread Chutney over top and sprinkle with chopped green onions. Serve with crackers.

MAKES 2 CUPS

A "bunch" of green onions = 1/2 cup
A "bunch" of herbs = 1 cup chopped herbs

Grow your own green onions by planting any leftover in your garden. Leftover green onions (in any condition) may be planted in the garden; just lop off the tops and poke a hole in the dirt, firming up the soil around the onion. Voila! you have one less trip to the store in the future when you just need a snip. They will multiply over time, too.

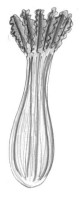

anne's stuffed celery

NANCY ETHERIDGE

4 ounces blue cheese or Gorgonzola
8 ounces cream cheese
1 teaspoon chopped onion
1 clove garlic, put through a garlic press

With a little milk, beat together blue cheese,
cream cheese, onion and garlic until mixture
reaches spreading consistency. Spread in
celery sticks, or endive. Sprinkle with paprika.

MAKES 1 1/2 CUPS OF STUFFING

sidney's favorite pimiento cheese rolls

ESTHER GLOVER

12 frozen biscuits
Flour
2 cups Pimiento Cheese (see recipe page 46)

Arrange frozen biscuits, with sides touching,
in 3 rows of 4 biscuits on a lightly floured
surface. Let stand 30-45 minutes or until
biscuits are thawed, but cool to the touch.
Sprinkle thawed biscuits lightly with flour.
Press biscuit edges together and pat to form
a 10 x 12-inch rectangle of dough.
Spread evenly with Pimiento Cheese.
Roll up, starting at one long end; cut into
12 (about 1-inch thick) slices. Place one slice
into each of 12 lightly greased 3-inch muffin
pan cups. Bake at 375° for 20 to 25 minutes
or until golden brown. Cool slightly and
remove from pan.

MAKES 12 ROLLS

*This was an instant hit — not just
because it contains pimiento cheese!
You can also make cinnamon rolls from
the same recipe, substituting butter,
brown sugar, and cinnamon for
the cheese. They're great, too!*

felix's chili con queso (pretty much)

GAY ESTES

I tablespoon vegetable oil
I large onion, chopped
Salt and pepper to taste
I clove garlic
1/4 teaspoon cayenne
2 tablespoons paprika
I 1/2 teaspoons sugar
1/4 cup flour
2 tablespoons chili powder
I can (8 ounce) tomatoes with
   chiles or canned tomatoes
1/2 pound American or
   mild cheddar cheese, grated

Simmer oil, onion, salt and pepper, tomatoes, cayenne, sugar, and paprika in a heavy pot about 25-30 minutes. Mix flour and water and add to mixture, stirring until smooth and thick. Add cheese, stirring constantly to prevent sticking and cook over low heat until well blended and smooth. Serve with tortilla chips.

MAKES 4 CUPS

susie's hearty queso

BETTY DAVIS

I pound spicy bulk sausage
   (Jimmy Dean or Owens hot)
2 pounds Velveeta cheese
I teaspoon garlic powder
I can cream of mushroom soup
Crushed red pepper
I pound ground beef
3 tomatoes, chopped
I tablespoons Tabasco
I cup chopped onion

Melt cheese in double boiler. Brown meats in skillet and add to cheese. Sauté onions till soft, add to cheese. Add other ingredients. Serve hot with chips.

MAKES 8 CUPS

creamy jalapeño dip

NANCY KEELY

24 ounces cottage cheese, small curd
2 tablespoons lemon juice
2 pickled jalapeños, chopped fine
Salt and pepper to taste
1 heaping tablespoon mayonnaise
1 bunch green onions, chopped
1 tablespoon pickled jalapeño juice

Combine and serve with corn chips.

MAKES 3 CUPS

*For a smoother consistency,
whirl in blender before serving.*

cheddar carousel

BETTY DAVIS

1 pound sharp cheddar cheese, grated
1 medium onion, grated
1/2 teaspoon Tabasco
3/4 cup mayonnaise
1 clove garlic, minced
1 cup chopped pecans
Roasted Raspberry Chipotle Sauce
   (available at most grocery stores)

Combine all ingredients except raspberry
sauce, and mix well. Place in mold lined
with plastic wrap. Chill thoroughly.
Unmold and spread with raspberry sauce.

SERVES 10

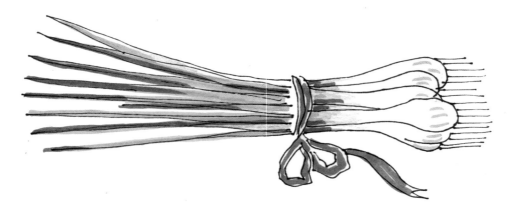

pancho villa pie

ANNE HAWKINS

2 cans (16 ounce) refried beans
3 avocados, mashed with
   lime juice and salt and pepper
1 cup mayonnaise
1 cup sour cream
1 package Taco Seasoning
1 1/4 cups cheddar cheese, grated
1 1/4 cups Monterrey jack cheese, grated
1-2 tomatoes, diced
1 jar (3 ounce) black olives, sliced
1 cup of cilantro, chopped

In an 8 x 8-inch serving dish, spread layer of refried beans. Make a second layer of avocado mixture. Combine mayonnaise and sour cream and spread to make third layer. Generously sprinkle taco seasoning over all to make fourth layer. Spread at least 2 1/2 cups of a combination of cheddar and jack cheese. Top with diced tomatoes, sliced olives and cilantro. Serve with a spreader — this is too thick for dipping chips.

MAKES 10 CUPS

tomato cheese tartlets

MARIQUITA MASTERSON

3/4 stick butter, room temperature
1/2 cup flour
1/3 cup masa harina
1 1/2 tablespoons cold water
Salt and pepper, to taste

Combine above ingredients. Roll about a tablespoon of dough into a ball and flatten with the palm of your hand. (These will rise a bit so make them thin.) Press into bottom and sides of each tartlet. Bake at 375° for 15 minutes.

3 1/2 ounces grated sharp cheddar cheese
6 tablespoons butter
1/4 cup sour cream
1 egg
2 tablespoons chopped basil
2 tablespoons chopped chives
3 medium Roma tomatoes, sliced

Combine cheese, butter, sour cream, onion, egg, basil and chives. Spoon filling into shells. Top with 1 slice of tomato. Bake at 375° for 30 minutes.

MAKES 24 TARTLETS

tzatziki

MARGARET WOLFE

4 cups plain yogurt, whole milk or low fat
2 cucumbers peeled and seeded
2 tablespoon plus 1 teaspoon kosher salt
1 cup sour cream
2 tablespoons Champagne or
    white wine vinegar
1/4 cup freshly squeezed lemon juice
    (2 lemons)
2 tablespoons olive oil
1 tablespoon minced garlic (2 cloves)
1 tablespoon minced fresh dill
1/2 teaspoon freshly ground black pepper

Place yogurt in paper towel lined sieve and set over a bowl. Grate cucumber and toss with 2 tablespoons salt; place in another sieve and set over another bowl. Place both bowls in the refrigerator for 3-4 hours so the yogurt and cucumber can drain. Transfer thickened yogurt to a large bowl. Squeeze as much liquid from cucumbers as possible and add to yogurt. Mix in sour cream, vinegar, lemon juice, olive oil, garlic, dill, and 1 teaspoon salt and pepper. Allow to sit in refrigerator for a few hours for flavors to blend.

MAKES ABOUT 5 CUPS

Can be prepared days ahead of time. Great as a dip served with pita bread, or as an accompaniment to highly seasoned food.

cilantro mousse

MARIQUITA MASTERSON

2 envelopes unflavored gelatin
1/4 cup water
1 cup whipping cream
1 cup mayonnaise
1/4 clove garlic
1 tablespoon grated onion
1 bunch cilantro
1 small jalapeño
1 tablespoon chicken flavor bouillon

Put 1 cup of cold water in saucepan. Stir in gelatin. Cook over low heat until all gelatin is dissolved. Set aside. In blender, mix cream, mayonnaise, garlic, onion, cilantro, jalapeño, and bouillon. Add bloomed gelatin and mix. Pour into a 3 cup mold greased with mayonnaise and chill thoroughly. Unmold onto serving plate and garnish with parsley and lemon slices. Serve with crackers or as a side dish.

MAKES 3 CUPS

sylvia bartz'
avocado mousse

SYLVIA BARTZ' AVOCADO MOUSSE

BETTY DAVIS

2 envelopes unflavored gelatin
1/4 cup cold water
1 cup parsley
2 green onions
4 ripe avocados
3 tablespoons lemon juice
1 teaspoon powdered bouillon
1/2 cup water
1 cup mayonnaise
1/8 teaspoon hot sauce
1 cup sour cream
1/2 teaspoon dried dill
1/4 teaspoon salt

Soften gelatin in 1/4 cup cold water and place in warm water bath to dissolve. Mince parsley in food processor. Add green onions and avocado and puree. Add lemon juice, then with processor running, add gelatin. Add 1/2 cup water with bouillon dissolved in it. Add mayonnaise and sour cream, dill, salt and pepper. Blend well. Pour into a 4 cup mold greased with mayonnaise. Cover and chill. Invert onto serving plate and serve with good crackers.

SERVES 8-10

easy corn dip

LAURIE LIEDTKE

2 cans corn, drained
1 package (8 ounce) cream cheese
1 teaspoon red pepper
2 teaspoon cumin
1 can (7 ounce) diced green chiles, drained

Mix all ingredients together. Heat and serve with corn chips.

MAKES ABOUT 4 CUPS

mexicorn dip
MARGARET ROTAN

3 cans (7 ounce) Mexicorn, drained
1 stick Cracker Barrel Sharp Cheese, grated
3 tablespoons mayonnaise
Cayenne pepper, to taste
1 bunch green onions (green and white parts)

Make one day ahead. Combine and mix well.
Taste for seasoning. Best served with blue
corn tortilla chips.

MAKES ABOUT 2 CUPS

frances' baked sweet onion dip
LUCY CHEADLE

1/3 part mayonnaise
1/3 part chopped sweet 1015 onions
   (finely chopped)
1/3 part grated Swiss cheese

Mix, pour a thin layer, no more than 1/2
inch thick, into baking dish and cook at 350°
until browning and bubbling on top. Serve
with homemade whole wheat Melba toast.

This is a crowd-pleaser, so make plenty!

santa barbara "caviar"
ESTHER GLOVER

I can (15 ounce) black-eyed peas,
 rinsed, and drained
I can (15 ounce) black beans,
 rinsed and drained
I tablespoon minced garlic
1/2 small sweet onion, minced
1/2 small red bell pepper, minced
1/4 cup chopped fresh cilantro
I can (4 ounce) chopped green chiles,
 drained
3 tablespoons chopped fresh jalapeños
3 tablespoons fresh lime juice
2 teaspoons olive oil
I teaspoon salt
Pepper, to taste
I avocado

Combine the peas, beans, garlic, onion,
bell pepper, cilantro, green chiles, jalapeño,
lime juice, olive oil, salt, and pepper in a
bowl and mix well. Chill, covered, for
3 to 12 hours. Chop avocado and stir into
pea mixture just before serving. Serve with
tortilla chips.

MAKES 5 CUPS

green chile dip
LYDIA CAFFERY HILLIARD

I package (8 ounce) cream cheese, softened
1/2 cup mayonnaise
1/2 cup small curd cottage cheese
1/2 teaspoon garlic salt
2 teaspoons fresh chives, finely chopped
4 ounces canned green chiles, chopped
 (no seeds)

Mix the cream cheese, mayonnaise,
cottage cheese, and garlic salt in a blender.
Stir in chives and green chiles. Serve with
corn chips.

MAKES ABOUT 3 CUPS

*Or, for a tasty lettuce wrap, spoon "caviar"
onto fresh lettuce leaves and roll.*

mold marcel

RROSE SÉLAVY

1 stick unsalted butter, softened
4 ounces Roquefort cheese, softened
3 ounces cream cheese, softened
1/3 cup finely chopped walnuts
2 tablespoons Cognac or brandy

In a medium bowl, thoroughly combine butter, Roquefort, and cream cheese. Stir in walnuts and Cognac. Can be molded or shaped. Use immediately or cover and refrigerate. Let soften for about 30 minutes before serving on endive spears.

MAKES 1 1/2 CUPS

asian nuts

MEG TAPP

1 pound walnuts
5 tablespoons tamari sauce
2 teaspoons chili sauce
1 1/2 tablespoons cooking oil
1/2 teaspoon salt

Mix ingredients and place on non-stick cookie sheet. Bake in a 350° oven, stirring twice, for 10 minutes.

MAKES 2 CUPS

blue, blue cheesecake

PRISCILLA PARSLEY

16 ounces cream cheese
3 cups blue cheese, crumbled, divided
2 cups sour cream, divided
1/4 cup green onions, sliced thin
White pepper
3 eggs

Beat cream cheese and 2 cups blue cheese in large mixing bowl until light and fluffy — about five minutes. Mix in 1 cup sour cream and 1/3 teaspoon white pepper. Add eggs, one at a time, mixing well after each addition. Pour mixture into buttered 9 inch spring-form pan. Bake 60-65 minutes at 300° or until toothpick comes out clean. Remove from oven, let stand 5 minutes. Mix 1 cup sour cream with 1 cup blue cheese and spread over top. Return to oven for 5 minutes. Cool completely. Refrigerate several hours or overnight. To serve, place on serving plate. Carefully remove sides of pan. Garnish top with green onions. Serve with Melba toast.

MAKES 1 9-INCH CHEESECAKE

green herb dip

NANCY ETHERIDGE

8 ounces cream cheese at room temperature
1/2 cup sour cream at room temperature
1/2 cup mayonnaise
3/4 cup chopped green onions
   white and green parts (about 3)
1/4 cup chopped fresh parsley
1 tablespoon fresh dill
1 teaspoon kosher salt
1/4 teaspoon freshly ground black pepper

Put all ingredients in food processor.
Pulse 10-12 times until just blended but
not pureed. Serve at room temperature.

MAKES 3 CUPS

Great with crackers or crudités.

spartan cheese

HELENA TROY

1 clove garlic, crushed
8 ounces cream cheese
1/4 cup plain yogurt or
   sour cream or half and half
2 ounces crumbled feta cheese
1 tablespoon fresh lemon juice
1/4 cup chopped fresh parsley
1/4 cup chopped green onion
1 tablespoon chopped fresh mint
2 teaspoon chopped fresh oregano
Pinch of nutmeg and cinnamon
Salt as needed

Bring all ingredients to room temperature
and combine in mixer (not blender or
processor). Taste for salt and allow time
for flavors to blend. Serve with crackers.

MAKES 2 CUPS

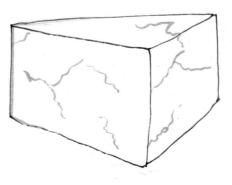

sarah's tortilla rollups

SARAH BERGNER

10-12 large flour tortillas
4 ounces Roquefort or Gorgonzola cheese
1/2 cup chopped fresh parsley or basil
1/4 cup or more chopped, oil packed,
  sun-dried tomatoes
8 ounces cream cheese
2 ounces chopped walnuts
A little sour cream, if necessary

Mix all ingredients and spread on flour
tortillas, roll up and chill. To serve, cut in
bite-size rounds and spear with toothpicks.
Good dipped in pesto or hot sauce.

MAKES 5 ROLLUPS

teresa's salmon mold

VIRGINIA WATT

1 package (8 ounce) smoked salmon,
  chopped
3 ripe avocados
1/2 cup croutons, crumbled
1/2 lemon, juiced
Champagne Vinaigrette dressing
  (see page 42)
Chives

Mix salmon, croutons, salt and pepper, and
dressing to taste. In separate bowl, squeeze
lemon juice over diced avocado. In a 2-cup
mold, layer salmon, then avocado, salmon
and end with avocado. Chill and unmold
onto serving plate and garnish with chives.

MAKES 2 CUPS

*This is great with crackers,
cocktail rye bread or crudités.*

salmon pizza

MARY HAYES

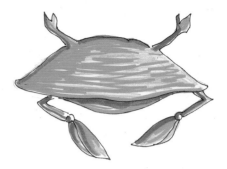

1 thin 12-inch pizza crust
8 ounces smoked salmon
8 ounces whipped cream cheese
3 tablespoons capers
Fresh dill
1/4 cup fresh lemon juice
Freshly ground pepper

Place pizza crust in 350° oven for
5-7 minutes to crisp. Remove and cool.
Mix cream cheese, lots of chopped dill,
capers, lemon juice and pepper and spread
on cooled pizza crust. Layer salmon on top
to cover. Cut into wedges and sprinkle with
more dill, capers and pepper. Garnish with
dill sprigs and lemon wedges.

SERVES 4

Try frozen pizza dough, or make your own.
Also great on pita bread,
English muffins, or flour tortillas.

hot crab dip

LINDA GRIFFIN

8 ounces cream cheese
1 tablespoon milk
8 ounces fresh lump crab
   (Do not use the giant lump)
2 tablespoons finely chopped onion
1/2 teaspoon horseradish
1/4 teaspoon salt
Dash of pepper

Mix all ingredients, except crab. Fold crab
in gently to keep pieces intact, if possible.
Cook at 350° for 15 minutes. Can be made
a day ahead and refrigerated. Reheat in
350° oven for about 20 minutes.

MAKES 2 CUPS

smoked trout dip

ESTHER GLOVER

1/2 pound smoked trout
3/4 cup mayonnaise
3 tablespoons chopped fresh dill
2 tablespoons horseradish, drained

Discard skin from trout, break into pieces
and put in bowl of food processor. Pulse
until finely chopped. Stir in remaining
ingredients. Add salt and pepper to taste.
Serve with carrot and celery sticks or
crisp toast.

MAKES 1 1/2 CUPS

cheesy spinach squares

ELLEN MORRIS

2 eggs beaten
1 cup milk
1 pound Monterrey jack cheese
  cut in 1/2 inch cubes or grated
1 cup flour 1 teaspoon salt
1 teaspoon baking powder
1 box (10 ounce) frozen chopped spinach
Parmesan cheese for topping
Paprika

Mix all ingredients in bowl. Put in 10 x 13-
inch greased baking dish with sides.
Sprinkle with Parmesan cheese and paprika.
Bake at 350° until cheese bubbles, about
20 minutes. Cut into squares when cool.

MAKES 24 SQUARES, DEPENDING ON SIZE

great balls of fire

NANCY KEELY

8 ounces extra sharp cheese, shredded
1 pound ground spicy sausage
2 cups Bisquick
Tabasco to taste

Mix ingredients, shape into small balls,
and bake at 400° till brown. Freezes well.

MAKES 24 SERVINGS

rosemary pecans

LYNN RAFFERTY

2 1/2 tablespoons melted butter
  (can use olive oil half and half)
3 tablespoons finely chopped fresh rosemary
  (or more)
1 teaspoon salt
1/2 teaspoon cayenne pepper
2 cups pecan halves or chopped walnuts

Melt butter; add salt, pepper, and rosemary.
Add pecans and toss well. Spread over a foil
lined pan or cookie sheet. Bake at 350° for
10-12 minutes.

MAKES 2 CUPS

olive cheese balls

LUCY CHEADLE

1 pound sharp cheddar cheese, grated
1 cup flour
Dried red pepper to taste
Freshly grated garlic to taste
Worcestershire sauce to taste
Large jar small-sized stuffed olives, drained

Grate cheese on coarse end of grater.
Let cheese soften at room temperature
until consistency of butter. Add flour
and seasoning, and mix into a dough.
Press mixture around olives and roll into
a ball with the olive in the center. Bake on a
greased baking sheet for 10 minutes at 400°.
Best hot, but good cold.

MAKES 24 SERVINGS

Try this with jalapeño stuffed olives.

cheese krispies

BETTY DAVIS

1 pound soft butter
24 ounces grated cheddar cheese
1 teaspoon cayenne pepper
1 teaspoon salt
4 cups flour
4 cups Rice Krispies

Slightly toast Rice Krispies in a 350° oven.
Cream butter and cheese. Add salt and
cayenne pepper, flour and Rice Krispies.
Form into walnut size balls, put on
cookie sheet and flatten. Bake at 350°
for 20 minutes.

MAKES ABOUT 18 DOZEN COOKIES

These freeze well.

longhorn pecans

TERRY DALTON

2 large egg whites
1 1/2 teaspoons salt
3/4 cups sugar
2 teaspoons Worcestershire Sauce
2 tablespoons paprika
1 1/2 teaspoons cayenne pepper
4 1/2 cups pecan halves
6 tablespoons unsalted butter,
   melted and cooled

Beat egg whites and salt till foamy.
Add sugar, Worcestershire, paprika, and
cayenne. Fold in pecans and melted butter.
Spread pecans evenly on a baking sheet.
Bake 30 to 40 minutes in a 325° oven,
stirring every 10 minutes. Remove from
oven and cool. Do not over brown; nuts
will become crisp when cooled. Store in
airtight container.

MAKES 5 CUPS

These are the best.
Good in salads or just to nibble!

ledbetter cheese straws

SARA LEDBETTER

1 pound grated sharp cheddar cheese
1 stick butter
2 cups sifted flour
1/2 to 1 teaspoon cayenne pepper

Mix the butter and cheese together in a food processor until creamy. Mix with flour and cayenne pepper. Use a cookie press or pipe onto a cookie sheet. Bake at 425° for 8-10 minutes.

MAKES ABOUT 24 CHEESE STRAWS

herbed potato chips

MARIQUITA MASTERSON

1 large bag potato chips
1/3 cup olive oil
3 tablespoons chopped chives
3 tablespoons chopped parsley

Mix oil, chives, and parsley and let stand for 30 minutes. Put potato chips on baking pan and drizzle with oil mixture. Bake 10 minutes at 350°.

MAKES ABOUT 6 SERVINGS

crowd pleasers

Chicken Vindaloo	Vegetable Salad
Porky's Chili	Brie Quiche
Taco Soup	Shelby's Refrigerator Rolls
Chicken Tortilla Soup	Bran Muffins
Oven Fried Chicken	Meyer Lemon Muffins
Open Sesame Chicken	Wayside Bread
Katy's Favorite Pork Tenderloin	Cheese Grits
Grilled Pork Tenderloin	Tomato Cheese Tartlets
Mint Jasmine Rice	Cilantro Mousse
Traveling Asparagus	Macaroni and Cheese

chicken vindaloo

ESTHER GLOVER

1/3 cup white wine vinegar
5 large garlic cloves, peeled
3 tablespoons fresh ginger, grated
1 1/2 tablespoons curry powder
2 teaspoons ground cumin
3/4 teaspoon ground cardamom
1/4 teaspoon ground cloves
1/4 teaspoon (generous)
    dried crushed red pepper
2 tablespoons yellow mustard seeds
2 pounds skinless, boneless chicken
    (thighs are fine)
4 tablespoons olive oil
2 1/2 cups chopped onions
1 can (14-16 ounce) diced tomatoes in juice 1
cinnamon stick
1/2 cup chopped fresh cilantro

Place first 8 ingredients in blender. Add 1 tablespoon mustard seeds and blend until smooth. Transfer spice mixture to large bowl. Add chicken and 2 tablespoons oil and toss to coat well. Heat remaining 2 tablespoons of oil in heavy, large pot over medium-high heat. Add onions and sauté until golden, about 5 minutes. Add chicken mixture and stir 3 minutes to blend flavors. Add tomatoes with their juice and cinnamon stick. Bring to boil and reduce heat. Cover and simmer until chicken is tender, stirring occasionally, about 30 minutes. Season chicken mixture to taste with salt and pepper. Mix in remaining 1 tablespoon mustard seeds. Simmer uncovered until liquid is slightly thickened, about 8 minutes. Stir in cilantro and serve over basmati rice.

SERVES 6

Freezes beautifully.
Quadruples for a crowd.
Goes well with Naan bread and a salad.

porky's chili

SIDNEY FAY

1/4 cup olive oil
2 onions, chopped
5 cloves garlic, chopped
2 1/2 pounds pork butt or tenderloin
  (cooked on the grill is best) cubed
1/3 cup chili powder
1 1/2 tablespoons ground cumin
1 1/2 tablespoons oregano
1/2 teaspoon cayenne
1 1/2 tablespoons salt
1 can (16 ounce) tomatoes
3 cups chicken broth
2 cans black beans
1 cup cheddar cheese
1/2 cup green onions

Heat oil and cook onions and garlic.
Stir in spices, tomatoes, chicken broth,
and pork. Simmer 1 1/2hours. Add beans
and cook for additional 15 minutes.
Serve with cheese and green onions on top.

SERVES 6

taco soup

DEBBIE ROBINSON

1 pound ground beef
1 onion, chopped
1 green pepper, chopped
1 can (7 ounce) corn, drained
1 can (10 ounce) tomatoes with chiles
1 can (16 ounce) pinto beans
1 package Taco Seasoning

Sauté ground meat in a little oil; add onion
and green pepper. Add other ingredients
and cook for 30 minutes. Add water or
cumin, if needed.

SERVES 4

Garnish:
Grated cheese, dollop of sour cream,
sliced avocado, tortilla strips
(see page 78) and cilantro.

Tear fresh cilantro instead of cutting
to avoid black edges.

chicken tortilla soup

SHELBY JONES

1 cup onion, chopped
1 avocado, chopped
2 teaspoons minced garlic
2 tablespoons vegetable oil
1 (4 ounce) can of green chiles, chopped
1 (15 ounce) can Italian-style stewed
    tomatoes, chopped, reserving the juice
4 cups chicken broth
1 teaspoon lemon pepper
2 teaspoons Worcestershire sauce
1 teaspoon chili powder
1 teaspoon cumin
1 teaspoon hot sauce, or to taste
4 tablespoons flour
1/2 cup water
1 pound boneless, skinless chicken breast,
    cut into small cubes
Salt and pepper to taste
Tortilla Strips (see right)
Sour cream
Cilantro

In a large saucepan, cook the onion and the garlic in oil over moderately low heat for 5 minutes, or until onion is softened. Add the chiles, tomatoes and their juice, broth, lemon pepper, Worcestershire sauce, spices and hot sauce, and simmer for 20 minutes.

In a small bowl, combine the flour with the water and whisk into soup. Bring the soup back to a boil and simmer for 5 minutes. Add the chicken and simmer for 5 minutes or until it is cooked. Add salt and pepper to taste. Stir in sour cream or reserve to dollop on top. Garnish with tortilla strips, chopped avocado, and fresh cilantro.

SERVES 4-6

Tortilla Strips

4 corn tortillas, cut into 1/4 inch strips
Non stick vegetable oil spray

Arrange tortilla strips in one layer in a baking pan sprayed with vegetable oil spray. Bake in 400° oven for 10 minutes until lightly toasted and crispy. Sprinkle lightly with salt, if desired.

MAKES ABOUT 1 CUP OF STRIPS

oven fried chicken

FRANCEY PENGRA

4 boneless chicken breast halves
1 cup sour cream or yogurt
1 teaspoon Dijon mustard
1 cup flour or 1/2 cup crushed corn flakes
2 teaspoon salt
1/4 teaspoon pepper
2 teaspoons paprika

Add Dijon mustard to sour cream or yogurt. Roll chicken in mixture to moisten. Combine flour, salt, pepper, and paprika. Throw a few chicken pieces at a time into the flour mixture and toss until pieces are covered. Put 1/2 cup butter into a 13 x 9-inch pan. Place in the heated oven and let the butter melt. Put the dusted chicken into the pan, skin side down, if you've left the skin on. Bake 30 minutes at 425° then turn over and bake another 30 minutes. Place on paper towels to cool and, bingo! Non-messy oven fried chicken.

SERVES 4

Great hot or cold!

open sesame chicken

SHERRY ZAHAD

3 pounds skinned, boneless chicken breasts (can be cut into strips)
2 teaspoons dried sage or thyme
1/2 cup buttermilk
3/4 cup bread crumbs
3/4 cup toasted sesame seeds
1/3 cup finely chopped fresh Italian parsley
4 tablespoons unsalted butter, melted

Marinate chicken in buttermilk, sage or thyme, and salt and pepper to taste for 2-3 hours, turning occasionally. Preheat oven to 350°. Stir together bread crumbs, sesame seeds, and parsley. Roll chicken in crumb mixture, coating well. Arrange chicken in shallow baking dish. Bake, basting with melted butter, until golden brown and done, 30-40 minutes. Serve hot or cold.

SERVES 6

katy's favorite pork tenderloin

KAREN TERRELL

I tablespoon finely chopped garlic
I tablespoon finely chopped sage
  (more to taste)
I 1/4 teaspoons sea salt
1/4 teaspoon freshly ground pepper
I tablespoon olive oil
I pork tender
I tablespoon canola oil

Mix garlic, sage, salt, pepper, and olive oil and rub well on pork tender. Brown tender in canola oil in a hot skillet over medium high heat. Transfer pork to oven and cook at 400° until pork reaches 145-150° on a meat thermometer. Let rest for 10 minutes before slicing.

SERVES 2

For larger servings, simply multiply recipe by number of tenderloins.

grilled pork tenderloin

MIMI KERR

2 large pork tenderloins
1/3 cup orange marmalade
3 tablespoons soy sauce
1/3 cup orange juice
I can beer
I tablespoon mustard
2 cloves garlic, minced

Combine beer, orange marmalade, soy sauce, garlic, mustard, and orange juice in a deep bowl. Submerge pork tenders in marinade, and let stand for at least an hour. Remove pork from marinade, reserving marinade and cook over open fire, turning frequently and basting with marinade. Or bake in a 450° oven for 20 minutes, then reduce heat to 350° and bake for 15-20 minutes more. Test for doneness. Place marinade in a saucepan and bring to a boil for a few minutes. Place cooked tenderloin in a baking dish, and cool. Pour marinade over tenderloin and refrigerate. Serve pork at room temperature, sliced in medallions with Herb Mayonnaise (recipe on page 89).

SERVES 4-6

mint jasmine rice

I cup jasmine rice
I tablespoon olive oil
I/2 cup onion, finely chopped
I/4 cup fresh mint, coarsely chopped
Grated zest of I lemon
I/4 cup fresh Italian parsley, coarsely chopped
I teaspoon kosher salt
2 teaspoons fresh lemon juice

Cook, rinse, and drain rice. Heat olive oil
and cook onion. In a bowl combine rice
and onion and toss with other ingredients.
Serve at room temperature.

SERVES 6

traveling asparagus

SAVANNAH GEORGE

Throw cleaned and washed asparagus spears
into a pot of boiling water. Cook until just
tender and drain. Put into a bowl of ice
water to cool, then wrap in a clean dishtowel
to dry and put in refrigerator. These can be
eaten cold or reheated.

Serve cold with Dad's Mayonnaise
(recipe on page 90) or Herb Mayonnaise
(recipe on page 89).

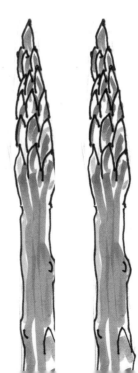

vegetable salad

NANCY KEELY

1 pound green beans, blanched and chilled
1/2 pound broccoli crowns, blanched and
   chilled
1 (14 ounce) can artichoke hearts
1/2 onion, chopped fine
1 cup Ranch Dressing

Mix thoroughly and chill at least 24 hours
before serving.

SERVES 4

brie quiche

DEBBIE ROBINSON

9 inch pie shell
8 ounces Brie, rind removed
8 ounces cream cheese
4 tablespoons butter
6 tablespoons cream
4 eggs, beaten
1 tablespoon minced onion

Bake pie shell for 12 minutes at 400°.
Combine other ingredients and pour into
shell. Bake for 25 minutes at 375°.

SERVES 4

shelby's refrigerator rolls

SHELBY JONES

1 cup boiling water
1/4 cup sugar
1 teaspoon salt
6 tablespoons shortening
1 egg, well beaten
3 1/2 cups flour
1 package dry yeast, dissolved in
    2 tablespoons warm water

Place boiling water, sugar, salt, and shortening in mixing bowl. Mix and cool. Add yeast mixture and egg. Mix in flour and beat well. Store in refrigerator, usually overnight. When ready to bake, roll out and cut. Dip in melted butter, fold over, and place on cookie sheet. Allow 1 1/2hours to rise before baking at 425° for 5 - 10 minutes. You can bake these until almost brown, wrap in foil and freeze. When ready to serve, heat in loosely wrapped foil for about 5 minutes.

MAKES ABOUT 24 ROLLS,
DEPENDING ON THE SIZE

bran muffins

NANCY ETHERIDGE

1 cup boiling water
1 cup Bran Buds cereal
1/2 cup unsalted butter
1 1/2 cups sugar
2 eggs (one at a time)
2 cups buttermilk
2 1/2 cups flour sifted with
    2 1/2 teaspoons baking soda
    1/2 teaspoon salt
2 cups All Bran cereal

Combine Bran Buds and boiling water and let cool. Cream together butter and sugar. Add eggs, one at a time and buttermilk. Combine with cooled Bran Buds; flour sifted with baking soda and salt; and All Bran. Cover and refrigerate. Batter keeps for one month in refrigerator. Bake in well-greased muffin pan at 400° for 25 minutes.

MAKES ABOUT 24 MUFFINS

meyer lemon muffins

MEG TAPP

2 cups flour
1 cup plus
  2 tablespoons sugar, divided
1 teaspoon baking soda
1 teaspoon salt
3 Meyer lemons, divided
2 eggs
1 cup milk
1/2 cup butter, melted
1/8 teaspoon cinnamon

Combine flour, 1 cup sugar, baking soda, and salt in a large mixing bowl and set aside. Cut two lemons into 1-inch pieces. Put them in a blender or food processor and pulse until finely chopped. Do not puree lemons. You will want to see bits of peel in the muffins. Combine lightly beaten eggs with milk, butter, and chopped lemon. Stir well. Make a well in the center of the dry ingredients and pour in the lemon mixture. Stir just until all ingredients are moistened. Spoon the batter into well-buttered muffin pans, filling each half full. Combine the remaining 2 tablespoons of sugar and the cinnamon. Sprinkle about 1/4 teaspoon over each muffin. Cut the remaining 1 lemon into 9 paper thin slices and cut each slice in half.

Top each muffin with a half slice of lemon. Bake about 20 minutes in a 400° oven until golden brown. Loosen muffins with a knife and remove from pan. Cool. Great warm or at room-temperature.

MAKES 18 MUFFINS

Meyer lemon trees are available at the Mart. Grow your own!

wayside bread

NANCY KEELY

3 cups self-rising flour
1/2 cup sugar
1 can beer
1 stick butter, melted

Mix flour, sugar, and beer and put into
greased loaf pan. Bake in 350° oven for
45 minutes. Pour melted butter over loaf
and bake for another 15 minutes.

This is so easy and really good.

cheese grits

MARIANNE CRAIN

4 cups cooked grits (instant grits are fine,
   longer cooking are better)
8 ounces grated cheddar cheese plus
   1 ounce of cheese for topping
2 tablespoons butter
Salt and pepper, to taste
2 tablespoons jalapeño, finely chopped
   (optional but really good)
Dash of paprika

Prepare grits in medium saucepan.
Remove from heat and add cheese, butter,
and jalapeños. Stir until cheese is melted.
Pour into buttered 2 quart ovenproof dish.
Sprinkle cheese then dust with paprika.
Run under broiler to melt cheese on top.

Variations: More cheese is even better.
Also, try picante or hot sauce.
You can add anything that
suits your fancy.

macaroni and cheese

GAIL HENDRYX

8 tablespoons+ unsalted butter

5 cups milk

1/2 cup+ all-purpose flour

1 teaspoon kosher salt plus

1/4 teaspoon freshly ground black pepper

1/4 teaspoon cayenne pepper

5 cups grated cheese (a combination of your
   choice i.e., cheddar, white cheddar,
   fontina, asiago, Parmesan, Gruyere,
   Monterrey Jack, or any flavorful cheese)

1 cup green onions, white and green parts,
   thinly sliced

5 ounces fresh goat cheese

4 cups macaroni, elbow or tubetti

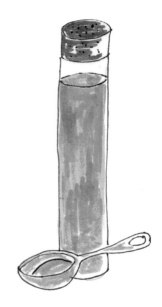

Warm the milk in a medium saucepan over low heat. Melt the butter in a large saucepan over medium heat. Whisk in the flour and cook for two minutes or until mixture is thick and smooth. Whisking constantly, gradually add the warm milk. Cook over low heat for 8 − 10 minutes, whisking occasionally. Remove from heat; add salt, pepper, and cayenne. Set aside 3/4 of a cup of the combined cheeses and 1 tablespoon of the green onions. Add the remaining 4 1/4 cups of cheese to the warm white sauce. Stir well until combined; add goat cheese and green onions. Set aside. In a large pot of salted water, boil the macaroni until done. Overdone is better than underdone. Drain in colander and rinse under cool water. Stir the well-drained macaroni into cheese sauce. Pour mixture into lightly buttered, 2 quart casserole, and top with reserved cheese and green onions. Bake at 375° for about 30 minutes. Serve hot.

Love is a fruit in season at all times, and within reach of every hand.

Mother Teresa

sauces

Mikey's Vinaigrette

Blood Orange Vinaigrette

Banana Mango Salsa

Tapenade

Herb Mayonnaise

Basil Mayonnaise

Sesame Mayonnaise

Chipotle Mayonnaise

Dad's Mayonnaise

Hot Mustard

Remoulade Sauce

Pesto

mikey's vinaigrette

LINDY NEUHAUS

1/4 cup onion, chopped fine
3 tablespoons fresh parsley
2 tablespoons chopped pimiento
I hard boiled egg, chopped
2 tablespoons chives
I I/2 teaspoons sugar
I teaspoon salt
1/2 teaspoon red pepper
1/3 cup vinegar
3/4 cup olive oil

Combine all ingredients (except oil) in a
bowl, and whisk in oil, a little at a time.

MAKES I 1/2 CUPS

blood orange vinaigrette

NANCY KURTZ

3/4 cup fresh blood orange juice
I tablespoon Dijon mustard
I tablespoon plus
    I teaspoon white wine vinegar
3/4 teaspoon red pepper flakes, crushed
I tablespoon whole mustard seeds
3 tablespoons olive oil
Kosher salt to taste

Stir together all ingredients except olive oil,
Whisk in oil in small droplets until
completely emulsified.

MAKES I CUP

*You can find blood orange juice at your
grocery store, but for fresher juice,
buy a blood orange tree at the Mart.
They grow well in Houston!*

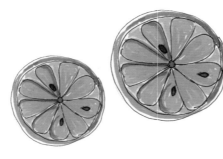

banana mango salsa

LUCY CHEADLE

2 bananas, chunkily chopped
1/4 cup cilantro, chopped fine
1/2 cup raisins, soaked in warm water
1 ripe mango, peeled and cubed
4 tablespoons fresh squeezed lime juice
1/2 teaspoon jalapeño, finely chopped
   (or a few dashes of Tabasco sauce)

Combine ingredients and gently toss.
Good as a fruit salad or salsa.

MAKES 2 CUPS

tapenade

ESTHER GLOVER

2 cloves garlic, peeled
2 cups pitted Kalamata olives
2 anchovy fillets, canned
1/4 cup fresh parsley

With food processor running, drop garlic
through food chute and mince. Add olives,
capers, anchovies and process till finely
chopped. Add parsley and pulse to combine.

MAKES 2 1/2 CUPS

*Serve this thick olive paste with crostini, stir into
pasta, use as a sandwich spread or pizza topping.*

herb mayonnaise

MIMI KERR

1 egg
1 tablespoon Dijon mustard
1/8 teaspoon white pepper
1/2 cup chopped mixed herbs and greens
   (Italian parsley, spinach, basil, chives)
1 tablespoon lemon juice
1/2 teaspoon salt
1 1/4 cup oil (1/2 vegetable–1/2 olive)

Using a food processor with a steel blade,
blender, or mixer, combine egg, salt, white
pepper, Dijon mustard, and lemon juice.
Process until egg is a creamy consistency
(about 7 seconds). With motor running,
slowly add oil in a thin trickle. As volume
increases, oil can be added at a faster rate.
Watch carefully to see that the oil has
been absorbed by the egg and there is
none floating free as you increase the oil.
Do not over-process. Add chopped herbs
and process for a few seconds. Store in
refrigerator for up to 3 days.

MAKES 2 CUPS

basil mayonnaise

HERB GARDINER

2 1/2 tablespoons white wine vinegar
1 large egg
1 1/2tablespoons whole grain mustard
1 tablespoon chopped fresh basil
1/2 teaspoon salt
1/2 teaspoon ground pepper
1 cup vegetable oil

Blend everything but oil in food processor. With machine running, add oil slowly until thickened. Refrigerate.

MAKES 1 1/2 CUPS

chipotle mayonnaise

SIDNEY FAY

1 cup mayonnaise
1/2 cup plain yogurt
2 tablespoons fresh lemon juice
2 cloves garlic
1/2 to 1 teaspoon salt
1-2 chipotle chile peppers,
   canned in adobo sauce

Combine in food processor until smooth. Chill.

MAKES 2 CUPS

sesame mayonnaise

SHERRY ZAHAD

1 whole egg
2 egg yolks
2 1/2 tablespoons rice vinegar
2 1/2 tablespoons soy sauce
3 teaspoons Dijon mustard
1/2 cup dark sesame oil
2 1/2 cups vegetable oil

Process egg and yolks, vinegar, soy, and mustard for one minute. With processor running, dribble in sesame oil then vegetable oil. Refrigerate.

MAKES 4 CUPS

dad's mayonnaise

LINDA GRIFFIN

1 egg
1/2 teaspoon salt
1/2 teaspoon mustard (prepared or dried)
3 tablespoons fresh lemon juice
1 cup vegetable oil

Put egg, salt, mustard, lemon juice and 1/4 cup oil in a blender and blend a few seconds. Add the rest of the oil, droplet by droplet until all oil is emulsified.

MAKES 1 1/2 CUPS

hot mustard

NANCY KEELY

1 cup brown sugar
3/4 teaspoon dry mustard
1 cup beef broth
3 eggs
3 tablespoons flour

Combine in top part of double boiler and
cook stirring until thick (about 10 minutes).

MAKES 2 CUPS

*Great on sandwiches or anywhere
you would use mustard.*

remoulade sauce

DOROTHEA FAUBION

1 chopped celery heart
1/3 cup chopped dill pickle
4 shallots, chopped small
2 cloves garlic
8 drops Tabasco
Fresh chopped parsley
2 tablespoons garlic wine vinegar
1/2 teaspoon Worcestershire sauce
1 pint mayonnaise
1 jar (5 3/4 ounce) Creole mustard
1/4 cup safflower oil

Mix ingredients in blender slowly adding oil
last. Mix well.

MAKES 4 CUPS

pesto

BETTY DAVIS

4 cups fresh basil
1/2 cup Italian parsley
4 cloves garlic
2 teaspoons pepper
3/4 cup virgin olive oil
1/3 cup lightly toasted pine nuts
1 1/2 teaspoons salt
3/4 cup grated Parmesan cheese

Place all ingredients except cheese in food
processor and pulse for about 5 minutes.
Remove to bowl and stir in cheese.
Can be frozen.

MAKES ABOUT 4 CUPS

*For cilantro pesto, use 4 1/2 cups fresh
cilantro in place of the basil and parsley.*

sweets

Lemon Squares

Lucy's Lemon Cream Tartlets

Microwave Pralines

Brittle Peanut Bars

Hot Fudge Sauce

Raisin Cookies

Mimi Kerr's Oatmeal Crisps

Oatmeal Cookies

Lace Cookies

Almond Lace Cookies

Ring-a-ling Cookies

Potato Chip Cookies

Danish Cookies

Mexican Chocolate Wedding Cakes

Bachelor Button Cookies

Sand Tarts

Terre's Fudge Pie

Good Luck Cookies

Triple Chocolate Cookies

Kelly-Mint Brownies

Disappearing Marshmallow Brownies

Double Fudge Brownies

Surprise Brownies

Mexican Chocolate Cake

Chocolate Angel Pie

Frisco Bars

Fruit Squares

Peanut Butter Fingers

Easy Sticky Rolls

Pie Crust

Hazel's Pecan Pie

New Zealand Pavlova

Buttermilk Sheet Cake with Praline Icing

Sour Cream Pound Cake

Easy Pound Cake

Banana Cheesecake

Apple Spice Cake

Pineapple Nut Cake

The Best Gingerbread

Carrot Cake

Blonde and Brunette Squares

lemon squares

ANNE TUCKER

I cup flour
2 teaspoons grated lemon zest
I/2 cup butter
2 tablespoons lemon juice
I/4 cup powdered sugar
I/2 teaspoons baking powder
I cup sugar
I/4 teaspoons salt
2 eggs

Mix flour, butter, and powdered sugar. Press in ungreased 8 x 8 x 2-inch baking pan, making I/2-inch edges. Bake 20 minutes at 350°. Beat granulated sugar, eggs, lemon zest, and juice, baking powder, and salt until fluffy. Pour into pan and bake about 25 minutes. Sprinkle with powdered sugar when cool. Cut into I inch squares.

MAKES ABOUT 48 SQUARES,
DEPENDING ON SIZE

Try this instead of powdered sugar:
1 cup confectioners sugar,
2 tablespoons fresh lemon juice,
1 1/2 teaspoons finely grated lemon zest
pinch of salt (optional).
Let stand for 10 minutes before
spreading over warm lemon squares.

lucy's lemon cream tartlets

LUCY CHEADLE

Dough:
I cup butter at room temperature
2 cups flour
6 tablespoons powdered sugar
Pinch salt

Mix above ingredients. Press very thin layer into mini tart pans. Form with thumb and make as thin as possible because it puffs when it bakes (almost doubles in thickness). Bake tart shells 8 - 10 minutes at 350°. Cool in pan. Turn out by lightly tapping pan upside down so that shells fall out. If you try to pry them out with a knife they'll probably break. Shells can be frozen at this point.

Filling:
8 ounces softened cream cheese
3/4 cup sweetened condensed milk
I/3 cup lemon juice
I tablespoon lemon zest
I teaspoon vanilla

Beat cream cheese and add the condensed milk slowly as you are beating the cheese. Add lemon juice, zest and vanilla as you continue to beat until the texture is creamy. Fill shells with lemon cream, chill and serve.

MAKES 12 SMALL TARTS

May be frozen and defrosted
on the way to the Mart.

microwave pralines

MIMI KERR

1 pound brown sugar
1 cup whipping cream
2 cups pecans
2 tablespoons butter
2 teaspoons vanilla

In a mixing bowl suitable for microwave oven, combine cream and brown sugar. Microwave on high 7 minutes. Stir. Microwave for 7 more minutes. Add butter, nuts and vanilla. Stir, and return to microwave for 1 1/2minutes. Using two spoons, one to spoon and one to push, drop pralines by spoonfuls on wax paper. Cool.

MAKES 24 PRALINES

brittle peanut bars

MARY GRACE HAMIL

1/2 cup butter
1 cup sugar
2 cups flour
1 cup peanuts, coarsely chopped

Cream butter and sugar; beat to mix well. Add flour and beat until dough holds together. Mix in 1/2 cup peanuts. Turn dough into unbuttered, 15 x 10-inch jelly roll pan. Press into thin layer. Sprinkle with other 1/2 cup nuts. Place wax paper on top and roll smooth. Bake 23-25 minutes at 375°.

MAKES 1 POUND

hot fudge sauce

KAY EBERT

1/4 cup butter
2 ounces unsweetened chocolate
1 cup sugar
1/2 cup evaporated milk

Melt butter and chocolate in double boiler. Stir in sugar and evaporated milk. Cook in double boiler for 10 minutes.

MAKES 1 1/2 CUPS

Makes anything taste better.

raisin cookies

DOROTHEA FAUBION

1 cup brown sugar
2 cups flour
3/4 cup butter, softened
1 egg
2 teaspoons baking powder
1/2 teaspoon baking soda
1 teaspoon lemon juice
1/2 cup currants
1 cup raisins
1 teaspoon vanilla or lemon extract
   or 1/2 teaspoon almond extract

Combine butter, brown sugar and beat till
creamy. Add the rest of the ingredients till
just combined. Place small amount of batter
on buttered pans and press with a fork.
Bake at 350° for 10 minutes.

MAKES 24 COOKIES

mimi kerr's
oatmeal crisps

DELBY WILLINGHAM

1 1/2 cups brown sugar
1 1/2 cups butter (at room temperature)
3 cups rolled oats
1 1/2 cups all-purpose flour
1 1/2 teaspoons baking soda

Place all ingredients in large mixing bowl.
Using your hands, combine ingredients until
there are no lumps of butter. Roll mixture
into small balls and place on ungreased
cookie sheets. Flatten gently with a small
fork, fingertips, or the buttered bottom of a
glass. Bake 10-12 minutes in a 350° oven.
Transfer cookie sheets to cooling rack and
let cool. Cookies will harden while they cool.

MAKES 60 COOKIES

oatmeal cookies

JULIA WALLACE

1 cup butter
1 cup brown sugar
1 cup sugar
2 eggs, well beaten
1 teaspoon vanilla
1 teaspoon baking soda
1 1/2 cups flour sifted with
1 teaspoon salt
3 cups regular oatmeal
1 1/2 cups finely chopped pecans

In mixer, cream butter, brown and white sugar, and add eggs and vanilla. Gradually add flour sifted with soda, salt, and mace. Add oatmeal and finely chopped pecans. Make walnut size balls with hands and press very flat on a greased cookie sheet. Bake in 350° oven until brown around the edges — about 10-15 minutes. Cool on cake rack.

MAKES ABOUT 48 COOKIES

lace cookies

SUSAN MICLETTE

1 cup Quaker Oats (Regular, not 5 minute)
1 cup sugar
3 tablespoons flour
1/4 teaspoon salt
1/2 teaspoon baking powder
1 stick butter
1 egg, beaten
1/2 teaspoon vanilla

Melt one stick of butter and pour over the dry ingredients. Add one egg — beaten — and vanilla. Cover cookie sheet with foil, shiny side up. Drop 1/2 teaspoons of cookie dough, leaving enough room for them to spread. Bake at 350° for 8 minutes or until light brown. Cool before removing from foil.

MAKES 36 COOKIES

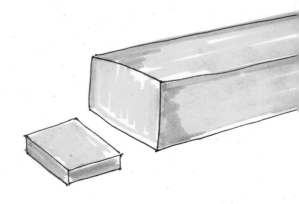

almond lace cookies

MARY NELL LOVETT

1 cup uncooked oatmeal
1 cup sugar
2 tablespoons flour
1/2 teaspoon salt
1/4 teaspoon baking powder
1 egg, slightly beaten
1 cup unsalted butter, melted
1 teaspoon vanilla
1 cup sliced almonds

Combine oatmeal, sugar, flour, salt, and
baking powder. In a separate bowl, whisk egg,
butter and vanilla. Add almonds and stir.
Line cookie sheet with foil and spray lightly
with cooking spray. Drop level teaspoons of
batter 3 inches apart. Flatten slightly.
Bake in a 325° oven until golden brown,
9-11 minutes. Let cool completely and
then peel off of the foil.

MAKES 36 COOKIES

 This is the best cookie ever!

ring-a-ling cookies

JOAN HOWARD

1 stick butter
3 tablespoons powdered sugar
1 cup flour, sifted
Dash salt
1 teaspoon vanilla
1 cup finely chopped pecans
Your favorite preserves

Cream butter and sugar, add salt to flour
and add 1/2 cup at a time to butter mixture.
Add vanilla and chopped pecans. Roll in balls
and place on a non-stick baking sheet making
an indention with your thumb in each cookie.
Put 1/2 tablespoon of preserves in each
indentation and bake at 300° for 20 minutes.

MAKES 18 COOKIES

potato chip cookies

CARRIE HORNE

1 pound margarine
3 cups flour
1 1/2 cups sugar
1/8 teaspoon salt
1 teaspoon vanilla
1 1/2 cups potato chips
1 cup chopped pecans
Powdered sugar

Combine margarine and sugar, cream
and set aside. Add vanilla, flour and salt
to sugar mixture. Stir in nickel-sized potato
chip pieces – do not pulverize. Add pecans.
Drop cookies on greased sheet, and press down
with fork. Bake at 325° for 12-15 minutes.
Sprinkle with powdered sugar while hot.

MAKES 60 COOKIES

danish cookies

FRANCEY PENGRA

2/3 cup finely chopped almonds
7 tablespoons butter
1/2 cup sugar
1 tablespoon flour
2 tablespoons milk
Orange zest

Combine in a large pot and cook over
medium heat until butter is melted. Remove
from heat. Drop by teaspoon onto greased
and floured baking sheet. Bake for 8 to 10
minutes on upper level of 325° oven.
Remove from oven and, while still warm,
fold each cookie over the handle of a wooden
spoon. Place on paper towels until cooled.
Store in an air-tight container.

MAKES 12 COOKIES

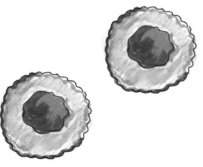

mexican chocolate wedding cakes

LUCY CHEADLE

3/4 cup firmly packed brown sugar
3/4 cup softened butter
3 ounces unsweetened baking
   chocolate, melted
1 teaspoon vanilla
2 cups all purpose flour
1 cup finely chopped pecans
1/2 teaspoon salt
Powdered sugar

In large mixer bowl combine brown sugar
and butter. Beat at medium speed, scraping
bowl often, until creamy (1 to 2 minutes).
Add melted chocolate and vanilla. Continue
beating, scraping bowl often, until well
mixed (1 to 2 minutes). Reduce speed to
low, add all remaining ingredients except
powdered sugar. Continue beating and
scraping bowl often, until well mixed.
Shape rounded teaspoonfuls of dough
into one inch balls. Place 2 inches apart
on cookie sheets. Bake at 350° for 8 to 10
minutes, or until set. Let stand 5 minutes;
carefully remove from cookie sheets.
Cool another five minutes. While cookies
are still warm, roll in bowl of powdered
sugar until entirely covered.

MAKES 24 COOKIES

bachelor button cookies

FRANCEY PENGRA

3/4 cup butter
1 cup brown sugar
1 egg, unbeaten
2 cups sifted flour
1 teaspoon baking soda
1/4 teaspoon ginger
1/4 teaspoon cinnamon
1/4 teaspoon salt
1 teaspoon vanilla
1 cup chopped nuts

Cream butter, add sugar gradually, and beat
well. Add unbeaten egg. Sift flour with dry
ingredients and add to butter mixture. Fold
in vanilla and nuts. Chill for several hours.
Make into small balls, dip in granulated
sugar, place on buttered cookie sheet, and
press down with a fork. Bake at 375° until
nicely browned.

MAKES 24 COOKIES

sand tarts

SIDNEY FAY

1/2 pound butter
1/2 cup sugar
2 cups sifted cake flour
1 cup chopped pecans
1 teaspoon vanilla
powdered sugar

Cream butter and add sugar. Add flour, nuts and vanilla. Shape into crescents and bake on ungreased cookie sheet at 325° for 20 minutes or until light brown. Roll in powdered sugar while still warm.

MAKES 4 DOZEN COOKIES

terre's fudge pie

MARGARET WOLFE

1 1/2 ounces unsweetened chocolate
1 stick butter
1/4 cup flour
1 1/2 cups sugar
3 eggs beaten
1/2 teaspoon vanilla

Melt chocolate and butter. Add to flour and sugar. Add eggs and vanilla. Bake in greased, 9-inch pie pan at 325° for 20-25 minutes. Top with whipped cream or ice cream.

SERVES 6-8

good luck cookies

FRANCEY PENGRA

1/2 cup butter
1 cup sugar
1 egg
1/4 cup molasses
2 cups flour
2 teaspoons baking soda
1 teaspoon salt
1 teaspoon cinnamon
1 teaspoon ginger
1 teaspoon ground cloves

Cream butter and sugar together and beat in egg and molasses. Sift together the flour, baking soda, salt, and spices. Stir dry ingredients into butter mixture. Chill dough 1 hour, or until it can be handled easily. Form dough into 1 inch balls and place on a greased baking sheet. Bake in a 375° oven for 10-12 minutes.

MAKES 24 COOKIES

triple chocolate cookies

ANNE HAWKINS

1/2 cup butter softened
3/4 cup granulated sugar
3/4 cup firmly packed brown sugar
1 teaspoon vanilla extract
2 eggs beaten
1 tablespoon milk
2 1/4 cups all-purpose flour
1/3 cup good cocoa powder
1 teaspoon baking soda
1/2 teaspoon salt
1 cup Semi-Sweet Chocolate Chips
1 (9 ounce) bag Hershey's Kisses

In a mixing bowl, beat butter, granulated sugar, brown sugar, and vanilla until well blended. Add eggs and milk. Beat well. In a separate bowl, stir together flour, cocoa, baking soda, and salt. Gradually add to butter mixture. Stir in chocolate chips. Shape dough into 1-inch balls. Place on an ungreased cookie sheet. Bake 10 minutes in a 350° oven. Cool for 1 minute, remove to wire rack, and press one Kiss in the center of each cookie.

MAKES 36 COOKIES

The Kisses make this cookie especially good!

kelly-mint brownies

ALMERIA COTTINGHAM

1 cup sugar
1/2 cup butter
4 beaten eggs
1 cup flour
1/2 cup pecans
1/2 teaspoon salt
1 can (16 ounce) Hershey's Chocolate Syrup
1 teaspoon vanilla
2 cups confectioners' sugar
1/2 cup butter
3 tablespoons Crème de Menthe (or more)
1 cup chocolate bits
6 tablespoons butter

Mix cake ingredients and pour into 9 x 13-inch greased, baking dish. Bake at 350° for 30 minutes. Allow to cool thoroughly. Cream together the sugar, butter, and Crème de Menthe, and spread evenly over the completely cooled cake. Put in refrigerator for a few minutes to let frosting harden. Melt chocolate bits and butter together in double boiler or heavy pot till smooth. Spread glaze on the frosted cake. Keep refrigerated, or better, in the freezer.

MAKES 12 SQUARES

disappearing marshmallow brownies

FRANCEY PENGRA

1/2 cup butterscotch pieces
1/2 cup butter
3/4 cup flour
1/3 cup brown sugar
I teaspoon baking powder
1/4 teaspoon salt
1/2 teaspoon vanilla
I egg
I cup miniature marshmallows
I cup semi-sweet chocolate chips
3/4 cup chopped pecans

Melt butterscotch and butter in a 3-quart heavy saucepan over medium heat, stirring constantly. Remove from heat and cool to lukewarm. Add flour, brown sugar, baking powder, salt, vanilla, and egg to butterscotch mixture in the saucepan. Mix well. Fold marshmallows, chocolate chips, and pecans into butterscotch batter just until combined, about 5 strokes. Spread into greased and floured 9-inch square baking pan. Bake for about 40 minutes in a 325° oven. Center will be jiggly but becomes firm upon cooling.

MAKES 12 LARGE BROWNIES

double fudge brownies

CAROLYN DAVIS

6 ounces unsweetened baking chocolate
I cup softened butter (salted)
4 large eggs
2 cups sugar
I tablespoon vanilla
1/2 cup all purpose flour
I cup mini semi-sweet chocolate chips

Combine chocolate and butter in a saucepan and melt over medium-low heat, stirring constantly until chocolate is just melted. Remove from heat and stir until smooth. In a large bowl, beat the eggs on medium speed until they are light yellow, about 5 minutes. Add the sugar and blend at low speed. Add vanilla and melted chocolate to the egg and sugar mixture. Add flour and mix thoroughly. Pour batter into 8 x 8-inch greased baking pan and level with spatula. Sprinkle mini chips evenly over top. Bake in the center of a 300° oven for 45-55 minutes or until a toothpick comes out clean. Do not over-bake. Cool to room temperature. Cover and refrigerate for at least I hour to make it easier to cut. Serve at room temperature or chilled.

MAKES 16 BROWNIES

surprise brownies

1 box of your favorite brownie mix…
or you could use the Double Fudge Recipe page 103.
Be sure to use the pan recommended in the recipe.
With half of the batter, layer the bottom of the pan.
On top of the first layer, put one of the following…
or your own concoction:

Hershey Symphony Bar
Unwrapped caramels
Peanut butter or peanuts
York Peppermint Patties

Top with remaining batter. Bake as directed.

Another variation:
Mix 3/4 cup brown sugar,
3 tablespoons butter and
3/4 cup pecans and sprinkle
    over top of batter.

Bake according to package or recipe
directions.

mexican chocolate cake

MEG TAPP

1 stick butter
1/2 cup vegetable oil
2 ounces unsweetened chocolate
1 cup water
2 cups all purpose flour
1 teaspoon baking soda
2 cups sugar
1/2 cup buttermilk
2 eggs beaten
1 1/2 teaspoons cinnamon
1 teaspoon Mexican vanilla

Combine butter, oil, chocolate, and water
in a saucepan and heat until chocolate is
melted. Add flour, soda, sugar, buttermilk,
eggs, cinnamon, and vanilla in a large bowl
and blend. Pour batter into greased 13 x 9-
inch pan and bake at 350° until cake tests
done, 20-25 minutes.

Ice with Mexican Chocolate Icing
(see right).

Mexican Chocolate Icing

1 stick butter
2 ounces unsweetened chocolate
6 tablespoons milk
1 pound powdered sugar
1 teaspoon vanilla
1/2 cup pecans (optional)

Combine butter, chocolate, and milk in
a saucepan and heat until bubbles form
around the edge. Remove from heat.
Add powdered sugar, a little at a time.
Add vanilla and beat until of spreading
consistency. Ice cake while still warm in pan.

SERVES 10–12

chocolate angel pie

FRANCEY PENGRA

2 egg whites
1/2 cup finely chopped walnut or pecan
  pieces (optional)
1/2 teaspoon vanilla
1/8 teaspoon salt
1/4 teaspoon cream of tartar
1/2 cup sifted granulated sugar
1 ounce German Sweet Chocolate
3 tablespoons water
1 teaspoon vanilla
1 cup cream, whipped

Beat egg whites with salt and cream of tartar
until foamy. Add sugar gradually, beating
until very stiff peaks hold. Fold in the nuts
(optional) and 1/2 teaspoon vanilla. Spread
in greased and floured 8-inch pie pan.
Build sides up to 1/2 inch above pan.
Bake in 300° oven for 50–55 minutes.
Cool. Melt chocolate and water over low
heat, stirring constantly. Cool until
thickened. Add vanilla, and then fold into
whipped cream. Pile into meringue shell.
Chill for 2 hours.

SERVES 8

frisco bars

BETTY DAVIS

Crust:

1/2 cup butter
1/2 cup sugar
5 tablespoons cocoa
1 teaspoon vanilla
1 egg lightly beaten
1 1/2 cups graham cracker crumbs
1 cup chopped walnuts

Place butter, sugar, cocoa, and vanilla in saucepan and cook, stirring until sugar is dissolved. Add egg and mix well. Remove from heat and stir in graham cracker crumbs and nuts. Pack into an 8 x 12-inch pan and refrigerate until cool.

Icing:

2 cups powdered sugar
1/2 cup soft butter
3 tablespoons Bird's Custard Mix
1 tablespoon milk
4 ounces semi-sweet chocolate

Combine powdered sugar, butter, Custard Mix, and milk, beating well. Spread over crust and refrigerate for 30 minutes. Melt chocolate in microwave for 2 minutes and spread over icing. Refrigerate again and cut into squares.

MAKES 10 SERVINGS

Betty says there is no substitute for Bird's Custard Mix. It is not always easy to find. It's imported from England by Kraft Foods and can be found in specialty food markets.

fruit squares

MARGARET WOLFE

Crust:

1 1/2 cups all purpose flour
1/2 cup confectioners' sugar, sifted
1/2 teaspoon salt
3/4 cup unsalted butter, cut in pieces

Combine flour, sugar, salt, and butter in food processor. Pulse about 30 times until the butter is the size of a small pea. Press mixture into bottom of ungreased 9 x 13-inch glass baking pan and about 1/2 inch up the sides of the pan. Bake crust at 375° for 10-12 minutes, or until it begins to brown.

Filling:

1/2 cup blackberry jam
(or your favorite fruit jam)
2 cups fresh or frozen blackberries
(or your favorite fruit)
2-4 tablespoons all-purpose flour

Melt jam in small saucepan over medium heat until liquefied. Mix blackberries with enough flour to fully coat and set aside.

Topping:

1/2 cup unsalted butter cut into cubes
1 cup all purpose flour
1 cup light brown sugar, packed

Combine butter, flour and brown sugar in food processor. Process until mixture comes together. Set aside. When crust is done, remove from oven and spread liquefied jam evenly over the hot crust. Sprinkle the berries and any flour remaining in bowl over the jam. Sprinkle topping evenly over the berries breaking up any clumps. Bake for 25-30 minutes or until brown and bubbly. Cool completely before cutting into squares.

SERVES 8-10

peanut butter fingers

ESTHER GLOVER

1 loaf white sandwich bread
1 (18 ounce) jar of creamy peanut butter

Cut crust off bread and cut each slice into
finger-sized pieces. Place crusts of bread and
bread fingers on cookie sheet and bake at
250° for 1 hour. Melt peanut butter with a
small amount of vegetable oil in skillet. Break
bread crusts up into crumbs. Coat each
finger in mixture and roll in bread crumbs.

MAKES A HANDFUL!

*Will keep for 2 months in airtight container …
but they never last that long!*

sticky rolls

FRANCEY PENGRA

1 cake of compressed yeast or
  1 packet active dry yeast
1 cup milk
3 tablespoons sugar
3 tablespoons shortening
1 1/2 teaspoons salt
1 unbeaten egg
3-31/2 cups all purpose flour
1/2 teaspoon butter
Brown sugar
1/2 teaspoon water
Cinnamon
Nuts

Soften yeast in 1/2 cup warm milk. Scald
1/2 cup milk and add 3 tablespoons sugar,
3 tablespoons shortening and salt. Cool to
lukewarm. Stir in egg and the softened yeast.
Add flour gradually and mix until well-
blended. Cover and let stand 15 minutes.
Grease and flour 2 muffin tins. Place
1/2 teaspoon butter, 1 1/2 teaspoons brown
sugar, 1/2 teaspoon water and nuts in each
pan. Divide dough in half. Roll into a slab
15-inches by 4-inches. Brush liberally with
butter and cinnamon sugar. Roll, starting
with the long side. Slice in 12 equal parts
and put in muffin tins. Repeat with the
remaining dough. Cover with a cloth and
let rise for 1 1/2hours or until the dough doubles
in size. Bake at 350° for 20-25 minutes.

MAKES 24 ROLLS

pie crust

BETTY DAVIS

1 cup Bisquick, or other
   all purpose baking mix
1/4 cup butter, softened
2 tablespoons boiling water

Mix baking mix and butter in bowl.
Add boiling water; stir vigorously until soft
dough forms. Press dough in a 9-inch pie
plate bringing dough to rim of pie plate
using fingers dusted with flour. Freeze for
15 minutes. Bake 8-10 minutes in a 400°
oven until golden. Cool for 30 minutes
before filling.

MAKES 1 9-INCH CRUST

*If you don't confess it's Bisquick,
they'll never know!*

hazel's pecan pie

CAROLYN DAVIS

3 eggs, slightly beaten
3/4 cup dark brown sugar
1 cup light corn syrup (such as Karo)
3 tablespoons melted butter
1 1/2 cups pecans, broken
Pinch of salt
Unbaked 9-inch pie shell

Beat eggs; add sugar, corn syrup, butter,
and vanilla. Beat. Add pecans and pour into
unbaked pie shell. Bake at 375° for about
8-10 minutes. Turn down to 325° and
bake for about 35 minutes more, until
browned and firm in the center. Let cool
before cutting.

MAKES 1 9-INCH PIE

This is yummy and not too sweet.

new zealand pavlova

CAROLYN DAVIS

Meringue:

2 egg whites at room temperature
1 1/2 cups sugar
Pinch cream of tartar (optional)
1 teaspoon vinegar
1 teaspoon corn flour
1/2 cup boiling water

Put all ingredients, except water, in a bowl
and beat on low speed until incorporated.
Increase speed to maximum and add boiling
water. Beat 15 minutes until thick and glossy.
Pile meringue onto cookie sheet lined with
parchment paper, shaping into a 7 inch
circle (or square, or heart, or whatever suits
your fancy) and bake in a 350° oven for
10 minutes. Lower temperature to 215° and
bake for 45 minutes or until the outside is
dry to the touch. Leave the meringue in the
oven to cool with the door closed. Remove
from oven and place meringue on serving
platter. Fill with custard (see right) then fruit.

Custard Topping: *(optional)*

1 cup heavy cream, whipped
2 egg yolks
1/4 cup sugar
Juice and zest of 1 lemon

Place egg yolks, 1/4 cup sugar and the juice
and zest of lemon into the top of a double
boiler and stir until thickened. Set aside to
cool. When cool, fold in whipped cream.
Pour custard into middle of meringue
and cover with kiwi fruit, strawberries,
passionfruit pulp, blueberries, or whatever
fruit you like.

SERVES 6

buttermilk sheet cake with praline icing

SARAH MCMURREY

2 cups sugar
2 cups flour
8 tablespoons butter
8 tablespoons vegetable shortening
1 cup water
1/2 cup buttermilk
1 teaspoon vanilla
2 eggs, slightly beaten
1 teaspoon baking soda

Sift sugar and flour together. Set aside.
Melt butter and vegetable shortening
together. Add water and bring to boil.
Remove from heat. Beat into flour-sugar
mixture. Add buttermilk, vanilla, eggs and
soda. Mix well and pour into buttered
11 x 18-inch pan. Bake 20 minutes at 400°.
Remove from oven and spread with
Praline Icing (see right).

Praline Icing

1 1/2 cups brown sugar
1 cup sugar
3 tablespoons butter
1 cup cream
1/4 cup chopped pecans
1 1/2 teaspoons vanilla

Combine sugars, butter, and cream in a
saucepan. Cook over medium heat to soft-
ball stage (236°). Remove from heat and cool
about 6 minutes. Add pecans and vanilla.
May be thinned with cream if it seems too
thick. Because it may harden, score cake for
slicing after spreading icing.

SERVES 8-10

sour cream pound cake

MIMI KERR

1 1/2 cups cake flour
  (can use all-purpose flour)
1 1/2 cups all-purpose flour
1/4 teaspoon salt
1/2 teaspoon baking soda
2 1/2 cups sugar
1 cup butter, room temperature
6 eggs
1 cup sour cream
1 teaspoon vanilla

Grease very well and lightly flour a 10-inch tube pan or bundt pan. In a mixing bowl stir together both flours, salt, and baking soda. In a large mixing bowl, beat the butter until light and creamy. Gradually add the sugar, beating until light. Add the eggs, one at a time, beating for one minute after each addition. Scrape the bowl often. Add vanilla and beat well. Add the dry ingredients and sour cream alternately, starting and ending with flour, beating after each addition until just combined. Pour the batter into prepared pan. Bake one hour at 325° or until skewer inserted into the cake comes out clean. Cool 15 minutes on a rack. Remove from the pan and cool.

SERVES 10-12

easy pound cake

BESSIE LIEDTKE

5 eggs at room temperature
2 cups sugar
1 tablespoon vanilla
2 sticks butter, room temperature
2 cups flour

Dump all together and mix for 10 minutes, scraping sides. Pour in greased, floured bundt pan. Bake for 70 minutes at 325°.

SERVES 8

banana cheesecake

MARIQUITA MASTERSON

1 baked 8-inch pie crust
12 ounces cream cheese
2 eggs
1/2 cup sugar
3 bananas

Beat together cream cheese, eggs and sugar. Add bananas and beat a little more. Pour into crust and bake 30 minutes at 325°. Chill and serve cold.

SERVES 6

apple spice cake
ADELE BENTSEN

1 1/3 cups vegetable oil
3 cups all purpose flour
1 tablespoon ground cinnamon
1 teaspoon baking soda
1 teaspoon salt
2 cups sugar
3 large eggs
2 cups apples (Granny Smith apples
   are good) cored and cut into
   1/2" pieces (leave peel on)
1 cup assorted nuts (pecans, walnuts),
   chopped (optional)
1 teaspoon vanilla

Sift together flour, cinnamon, baking soda,
and salt. Set aside. In a mixer with the paddle
attachment, combine oil, sugar, and eggs.
Mix on high speed until lemon yellow.
Gradually add flour mixture on medium
speed until just incorporated. Add apples,
and mix long enough for apples to break
down and add their liquid to the batter.
Add nuts and vanilla. Pour batter into a
12-cup bundt pan sprayed with cooking spray.
Bake in a 350° oven for 75-to-90 minutes or
until tester inserted in the center comes out
clean. Remove from oven and cool slightly on
wire rack. Invert cake; remove from pan and
cool, right side up, on rack.

This is good with or without the Caramel
Sauce (see below).

Caramel Sauce
1 cup light brown sugar
1/2 cup unsalted butter
1/4 cup evaporated milk
1 teaspoon vanilla
Pinch of salt

Combine ingredients in a small saucepan
over medium heat. Cook, stirring until
thickened to desired consistency.
Drizzle over warm cake.

SERVES 10-12

pineapple nut cake
LYDIA CAFFERY HILLIARD

2 cups flour
2 cups sugar
1 teaspoon baking powder
1 teaspoon baking soda
1/2 cup chopped nuts
2 eggs
1 can (20 ounce) crushed pineapple
   with juice

Combine all in one bowl. Mix and pour
into greased 13 x 9-inch pan. Bake about
35 minutes in a 350° oven. Cool and ice
with Cream Cheese Icing (see below).

Cream Cheese Icing

8 ounces cream cheese, softened
   Do not use non-fat
1 teaspoon vanilla
1 stick butter, softened
2 cups sifted powdered sugar

Put cream cheese, vanilla, and butter in
mixer bowl. Gradually beat in the powdered
sugar until creamy. Spread on cooled cake.

SERVES 10

the best gingerbread
MARIANNE CRAIN

3 eggs
1 cup sugar
1 cup molasses
1 teaspoon cloves
1 teaspoon ginger
1 teaspoon cinnamon
1 cup oil
2 teaspoons baking soda
2 cups flour

Place all eggs, sugar, molasses, cloves, ginger,
cinnamon, and oil in a bowl and beat well.
Dissolve 2 teaspoons baking soda in 1/8 cup
hot water and add to mix. Sift in flour and
beat well. Add 1 cup boiling water; beat
quickly and lightly. Batter will seem thin.
Bake in a 9 x 13-inch pan, sprayed with
cooking spray, for 45 minutes at 350°.

SERVES 8-10

carrot cake

FRANCEY PENGRA

2 cups flour
4 eggs
1 1/2 cup oil
2 cups sugar
2 teaspoons soda
3 cups carrots, shaved
2 teaspoons cinnamon
1 teaspoon salt
3 tablespoons rum extract

You may add a cup of chopped pecans to the batter. You may also add 1 teaspoon nutmeg. Bake in greased and floured bundt or cake pan for 45 minutes to 1 hour at 325°. Let the entire cake cool before icing.

Icing:

16 ounces cream cheese
1 box of confectioner's sugar,
   plus more if needed
1 tablespoon butter

SERVES 8

Add more confectioner's sugar if you like a less-creamy icing. I do.

blonde and brunette squares

CAROLYN DAVIS

1 cup firmly packed dark brown sugar
1 cup softened salted butter
1 large egg
2 teaspoons vanilla
2 cups flour
1/2 teaspoon baking soda
1 cup chopped pecans
1 1/2 cups semi-sweet chocolate chips

In a large bowl, blend the dark brown sugar and the butter at medium speed until well blended. Add egg and vanilla and beat at medium speed until light and smooth, scraping down the sides of the bowl often. Add the flour and baking soda, pecans and chocolate chips. Blend at low speed until just combined. Transfer batter to an 8 x 8-inch greased baking pan and bake at 300° on the center rack for 35-45 minutes until a toothpick comes out clean. Cool on a rack until room temperature and cut into squares.

MAKES 24 SQUARES

cool drinks

Lake George Tea-Ade

The Ultimate Lazy Tea

Cold Spiced Tea

Bulb Mart Limeade

Margarita Slush

Planter's Punch

Mart-tini

Mart Wine

Bay Breeze

Lemon Drop from the Citrus Booth

Brandy Freeze

Lake George Tea-ade

BO HAWKINS

In a one gallon pitcher put 7 regular size tea bags (decaffeinated is fine) and 20 sprigs of mint. Pour boiling water over to cover and let steep for 15 minutes. Strain into second one gallon pitcher and add 1 1/2 cups sugar and 1/2 cup lemon juice. Top off with water and stir. Pour into tall glass of ice and decorate with a sprig of mint.

MAKES 1 GALLON

The Ultimate Lazy Tea

SOMEONE'S DAUGHTER GAVE US THIS RECIPE, AND WE WERE SURPRISED HOW MUCH WE LIKED IT!

Open a one gallon container of bottled
  water, and pour out a few swigs.
Pour in 1 small tub of
  Crystal Light Peach Tea and 1 tub
  Crystal Light lemonade.
Shake and chill.

MAKES 1 GALLON

Cold Spiced Tea

SARAH MCMURREY

4-5 orange spice tea bags
1 1/2 quarts boiling water
2 cups cranberry juice or cran-raspberry juice

Brew tea, pour in pitcher and add cranberry juice. Serve over ice garnished with orange and lemon slices.

MAKES 2 QUARTS

Bulb Mart Limeade

ANNE TUCKER

1 (12 ounce) can of frozen limeade
   concentrate
1 (2 liter) bottle of Sprite Zero,
   lemon-lime flavor

Mix limeade and Sprite in a large covered pitcher. Refrigerate. Serve in tall glass over ice with a slice of lime.

MAKES ABOUT 2 LITERS

Adding tequila, vodka or rum works well, too!

Margarita Slush

SIDNEY FAY

Pour into a blender:
1 (6 ounce) can of frozen limeade
6 ounces of Gold Tequila
1 ounce Triple Sec

Turn on blender and add ice until the mix
has the consistency of a thick milk-shake.

SERVES 4 HAPPILY

Planter's Punch

À LA THE COMMANDER'S PALACE

1 1/2 ounces light rum
1/2 ounce grapefruit juice
1/2 ounce orange juice
1/3 ounce grenadine

Fill glass with ice and pour ingredients over.
Stir and serve with favorite garnish.

MAKES 1 COCKTAIL

Mart-tini

GAY ESTES

2 jiggers Tito's Handmade Vodka
1/2 jigger good limoncello

Garnish with a lemon slice or a sprig of mint.
Serve on the rocks, or if you prefer, straight
  up - shaken not stirred.

MAKES 1 COCKTAIL

Mart Wine

CARL ESTES

5 bottles (24.40 ml.) of dry white wine
4 cups of orange juice
2 cups simple syrup
2 cups brandy
1 cup Triple Sec
1 package passion fruit puree
2 thinly sliced lemons
1 pint strawberries
4 apples
4 oranges
4 peaches

Cut up the fruit and place all together in a
really BIG bowl. Pour chilled wine over fruit.
Serve chilled with a little fruit on the bottom
and a mint garnish.

MAKES ABOUT 36 SERVINGS

*Simple syrup is called for in several of our recipes.
Boil one part sugar to one part water. When sugar is
dissolved, remove from heat and cool.
Keep in refrigerator.*

*A fun fact, hummingbird nectar is made the same way,
just change the recipe to 1 part sugar to four parts water.
Clean feeder and change nectar every few days.*

Bay Breeze

SIDNEY FAY

6 ounces Caribbean rum
6 ounces frozen limeade

Place in a blender and add:
10 ounces of water
5 to 10 mint leaves
2 cups ice

Blend until ice is chopped and slushy.
Add a Myer's Rum floater.

MAKES 3–4 COCKTAILS

Lemon Drop from the Citrus Booth

MARGARITA LOBO

4 ounces lemon vodka
1 tablespoon powdered sugar
1 ounce Tuaca
1 ounce simple syrup

Shake in a cocktail shaker. Serve in a
frozen cocktail glass rimmed with sugar
and garnished with a lemon slice.

MAKES 1 COCKTAIL

Brandy Freeze

Combine two scoops of ice cream and a
jigger of brandy in a blender. Process until
mushy. Serve with a dusting of nutmeg on
top. A perfect after dinner drink or dessert.

MAKES 1 DRINK

The text in this little volume of recipes is set in Mrs Eaves. Designed by Zuzana Licko for Emigré Foundry, this typeface is inspired by Sarah Eaves, John Baskerville's wife. As Baskerville was setting up his printing and type business, Mrs. Eaves moved in with him as a live-in housekeeper, eventually becoming his wife. After John Baskerville's death, Sarah completed the printing of his unfinished volumes. While based on classic Baskerville typefaces, Mrs Eaves' overall lightness and openness give it a decided woman's touch.